SO-BZY-688

J-FICTION

Big Wish

Big Wish

BRANDON ROBSHAW

Chicken House

SCHOLASTIC INC. / NEW YORK

Copyright © 2016 by Brandon Robshaw

All rights reserved. Published by Chicken House, an imprint of Scholastic Inc., *Publishers since 1920.* SCHOLASTIC, CHICKEN HOUSE, and associated logos are trademarks and/or registered trademarks of Scholastic Inc.

First published in the United Kingdom in 2015 as *The Big Wish* by Chicken House, 2 Palmer Street, Frome, Somerset BA11 1DS.

The publisher does not have any control over and does not assume any responsibility for author or third-party websites or their content.

Library of Congress Cataloging-in-Publication Data

Names: Robshaw, Brandon, author.
Title: Big wish / Brandon Robshaw.
Description: First [American] edition. | New York : Chicken House/ Scholastic Inc., 2016. | "First published in the United Kingdom in 2015 as The Big Wish by Chicken House." | Summary: When a shooting star grants Sam a million wishes (as long as they are logically possible) he thinks that he will be able to make his life better at his new school—but he soon learns that you have to be very careful, because wishes can have unexpected consequences. | Description based on print version record and CIP data provided by publisher; resource not viewed.
Identifiers: LCCN 2015051396 (print) | ISBN 9780545904100 (hardcover : alk. paper) |
Subjects: LCSH: Wishes—Juvenile fiction. | Meteors—Juvenile fiction. | Conduct of life—Juvenile fiction. | Schools—Juvenile fiction. | Families—Juvenile fiction. | CYAC: Wishes—Fiction. | Meteors—Fiction. | Conduct of life—Fiction. | Schools—Fiction. | Family life—Fiction.
Classification: LCC PZ7.R56996 (print) | DDC 823.92—dc23
LC record available at http://lccn.loc.gov/2015051396

10 9 8 7 6 5 4 3 2 1   16 17 18 19 20

Printed in the U.S.A.   23
First printing 2016
Book design by Mary Claire Cruz

Chapter One

People often talk about having butterflies in their stomachs. Butterflies? With me it was . . . bees! Bats! Birds! Lobsters, snapping their claws!

It was a bright morning in early September, and I was decked out in my brand-new school uniform: dark gray trousers and blazer; white shirt; tie with diagonal red, black, and white stripes. New black shoes without a scuff on them. Two-day-old haircut. My Adidas shoulder bag had a new calculator in it, along with a collection of pens, a geometry set, and my lunch, which consisted of a ham salad sandwich, an orange, and a fruit-and-nut granola bar.

I was sitting in the kitchen, trying to eat my toast. The sun was streaming through the window, the radio was on, and the DJ sounded insanely cheerful. "Happy Monday, everyone!" and all that. It was okay for him. All *he* had to do was lounge around in a studio, play records, blabber on, and get paid buckets of money for it. He didn't have to go to a great big massive new school with a thousand kids in it.

All bigger than him.

"Are you all right?" my mom said. She always knows when I've got something on my mind. It's like she's telepathic. "Not too worried?"

"He should be!" said Maeve. "They'll eat him alive!"

Ben was so shocked, he stopped scratching his head. "Eat him alive? They'll go to prison if they eat him alive!"

"It's just an expression," Mom said. "Don't worry, Sam. They won't eat you alive."

"You don't know the place like I do, Mom," said Maeve. She finished there last year and she's about to start high school. "There are some real psychos."

"Be quiet!" said Mom. "Don't be so mean! Don't you worry about those psychos, Sam. Just keep out of their way."

"Oh, yeah, that's a really good idea, Mom," I said. Touch of sarcasm there, you know.

"Oh, come here!" Mom said, and she got up and hugged me, pressing me to her like I was a really little kid again. Only in those days my head only came up to her waist and now it was almost level with hers. And for a moment

I wished I *was* a little boy again, with nothing to do except swing on swings and dig in sand-boxes and play with my toys and eat candy and watch cartoons . . .

There was a knock on the door.

"That's Evan," I said.

He was standing there on the doorstep in his Mary Seacole Comprehensive School uni-form. It was his big brother's old uniform—the trousers ended way above his ankles, the sleeves of the jacket ended way above his wrists, and the jacket buttons didn't meet the buttonholes. Evan's a little overweight. Not actually *fat*. Just . . . well, he's in shape, and the shape is round, as my dad would say.

"What are you staring at?" Evan said. "Do I look really stupid?"

"No, no, no," I said quickly. "You look fine. Uber-cool."

"No need to be sarcastic." He sounded a little huffy.

I wished I'd kept my mouth shut. Except—a funny thing—now Evan looked so worried, I felt a lot less worried myself. I'd handed off the worry baton, like in a relay.

Mom came out into the hall. "Hello, Evan. Good luck, you two!"

Maeve appeared behind her. "They'll need it!"

"*You* survived it there, didn't you?" said Mom.

"Yeah, just about!" said Maeve.

Anyway, we set off up the street, me and Evan. Mom stood at the gate and called out, "Make some wise choices!" She's always said that, ever since I started elementary school. She thinks it's funny. But it's just annoying.

Parents don't always know the difference.

✱ ✱ ✱

Mary Seacole Comprehensive is a humongous new building. Mostly yellow, with steel girders on the outside, and between the yellow walls there are sheets of glass you can see the staircases through.

"Weird, isn't it?" I said to Evan as we stood outside. Hundreds of kids streamed past, jostling us as they went by. "We've gone from being the biggest kids to being the smallest kids."

"Yeah," said Evan. "Like in *Gulliver's Travels*. When he goes from Lilliput, where everyone's tiny and he's the giant, to Brobdingnag, where everyone's a giant and he's the tiny one."

Evan says stuff like that all the time. And he hadn't just seen the movie, either. He'd read the book, you could be sure about that.

"Yeah," I said. "I guess."

"But it's going to be okay," Evan said. "Remember what Mrs. Protheroe said—about the school's strict anti-bullying policy?"

"That's right," I said. "There's nothing to worry about."

We looked at each other. "Well," Evan said, "we'd better get in there."

We knew where to go. They'd shown us on Orientation Day. We were in Mrs. Protheroe's homeroom in Room 111 on the first floor. But there'd only been sixth-graders there then. It was all nice and quiet. Today it was like entering a giant beehive.

"You sure this uniform looks okay?" Evan said.

"Well, er, yeah," I said. "Totally."

"Your hair's sticking up."

"I know," I said. "I like it like that."

So we went in and found our way through

the noisy, crowded halls to Mrs. Protheroe's room, then went off to our first class, which was English with Mr. Swaledale, and do you know what? Nothing bad or scary happened at all.

Until recess.

Me and Evan were kind of ambling along the side of the blacktop, where some of the big kids were playing soccer. We were talking about who was the best ever Captain in *Captain Invincible*.

"Matt Lukovitz is good," I said. "He's funny. But I think I gotta say Garrett Butcher, on the whole, 'cause—"

"My dad says Sidney Kronk was the best."

This put me in a dilemma. I'd seen an old *Captain Invincible* episode with Sidney Kronk in it and I wasn't that impressed. But I didn't want to sound as if I was contradicting Evan's dad, who's really sick. He's been in and out of the hospital for the last two years, having all sorts of treatments and operations, and he can't work anymore. So I felt like it would be bad manners, if you know what I mean, to start saying that Evan's dad was all wrong about Sidney Kronk. Before I had a chance to figure out what to say, a soccer ball came whizzing toward us at about a hundred and fifty miles an hour and smashed Evan right in the face, knocking his glasses off.

"Hey!" shouted a really horrible voice. "Give us our ball back, you twerp!"

A tall kid with a pale face, black hair, and cold, hard eyes was glaring at us.

Evan was on his hands and knees looking for his glasses. Blood trickled from his nose. I picked up the glasses and gave them to him.

"The ball! Kick it here, you little jerk!"

"Aren't you even going to say sorry?" I said. "You just whacked him in the face."

"He should keep his ugly face out of the way, then!"

His friends were all laughing. But the boy himself didn't look like he thought it was funny at all. He started walking toward us. I threw the ball back, but he ignored it.

"What's your problem?" he said.

"You are." It just sprang to my lips. I knew it was suicidal, but it was *true*.

He opened his eyes wide. He was right in front of us now.

"You what? You *what*?"

He made a sudden movement with his hand like he was going to hit me. I jumped to one side, but then he casually moved his hand up and smoothed back his hair. His friends burst out laughing.

"Who are they letting in to this school these days? Look at these two doughnuts. *This* one"—he poked Evan really hard in the stomach, you could see his finger push right in—"is so fat, he couldn't get a uniform to fit him! And *this* one"—he poked me in the ribs and it really hurt—"has hair like a toilet brush. An orange toilet brush!"

His friends laughed even more and came closer, crowding around us. I gave Evan a kind of helpless look at the exact moment he turned and gave the exact same look to me.

"What's your name?" said the tall boy.

"Evan Carter," muttered Evan.

"What? Evan Farter?"

Cue gales of laughter from his friends. Evan went red.

"And you?" He turned on me. "What's your stupid name?"

"Why? What's yours?"

I don't know why I was acting like I had a death wish. I have this idea that life should be *fair*, you know? If he could ask me my name, why couldn't I ask him his? I know life *isn't* fair—grown-ups are always coming out with that one—but it *should* be.

There was a gasp from his friends. "You better teach him a lesson, Scorpus."

Scorpus gave a sneering grin—like a piece of string was pulling his upper lip up on one side. "Yeah, 'cause that's what school's for, ain't it? Learning lessons." He pushed me right back against the wall. I could feel the bricks scraping against my vertebrae. And I wished, more strongly than I'd ever wished for any-thing in my life, that I had superpowers, like in Marvel comics. If I was Spider-Man, I could punch him to the ground using all my spider-strength and then tie him up in a web. Or if I was the Incredible Hulk, I could hurl him right across the playground and he'd go splat against the far wall. Or if I was the Mighty Thor, I'd get out my hammer and—

"You gotta pay a *tax*," Scorpus said. "For being a wise guy. Give us your money."

"Leave him alone!" said Evan. "This school has an anti-bullying policy—"

Hurricane of laughter.

Scorpus held his hand out in front of me. "Lunch money."

"I haven't got any. I brought my lunch."

One of his friends—a thickset boy with a dyed-blond streak in his hair and a piercing in one of his eyebrows, even though that was against the rules—overturned my Adidas bag. The calculator, geometry set, and pens tumbled out, plus the lunch box.

"Oh, what we got here?" Scorpus picked

up the calculator and geometry set. "He's got all his little instruments—sweet or what?" He slipped them into his jacket pocket.

"Give those back!"

"Er, how can I put this? No." Then he opened the lunch box. "What've we got here? Ham salad? I hate ham salad." He dropped the sandwich and ground it under his heel, and all the salad came splurting out the sides. He threw the orange up and down a couple of times, then pulled back his arm and sent it whizzing right across the playground. It splatted on the wall on the far side, just like *he'd* have if I'd been the Incredible Hulk. Finally, he took the granola bar, looked at it, and slipped it into his other pocket. It was a chocolate-coated one.

"That's the end of the lesson," Scorpus said. "The lesson is, show some *respect*. You get me?"

All I had to do was say okay, or even just nod. But somehow . . . I just couldn't. I was scared of him. But I didn't respect him. So I just stared back dumbly.

"I *said*, d'you *get* me?"

"Oh, come on," said one of Scorpus's friends. "Let's play the game, the bell's gonna ring soon." He was a black kid with a shaved head, and even though he looked seriously tough, something in his voice gave me the idea he'd started to feel a little sorry for me.

Scorpus turned to look at him. "I'll 'come on' when I'm ready, all right?"

"Look—a teacher's coming!" Evan said.

I felt a surge of relief as I saw a bald teacher with glasses and a brown corduroy jacket walking our way.

Scorpus swore. "Okay, let's play soccer. You two"—he fixed us each with a laser-beam stare—"if you say anything, you're *dead*." He drew his finger across his throat. "Capeesh?"

"What?" I said. "I don't know what *capeesh* means."

Scorpus took half a step forward, and for a second I thought he was going to start on me again. But the teacher was close now. Shaved-Head pulled Scorpus's arm, and Scorpus finally slouched away.

"Whew!" Evan said shakily. "That was horrible!"

"What are we going to do?"

"Well . . . you can share my lunch."

"Thanks. But I meant, we'll have to tell, won't we?"

"Will we?"

"Yeah, Mrs. Protheroe said—"

"Yeah, but *he* said—"

"Yeah, but Mrs. Protheroe said—"

"Yeah, but he'll kill us!"

"He won't," I said. "They won't let him."

"How'd you know?"

"Look, they've got an anti-bullying policy. They have to, like, enforce it. Anyway, why should we let him get away with pushing us around like that and stealing my things? It's not fair!"

"Life's not fair," said Evan.

"Well, we'll have to try and make it fair, then," I said.

So we went to Mrs. Protheroe and dropped Scorpus right in the poop.

And dropped ourselves in it, too, as it turned out.

Chapter Two

When I got home from school, my mom asked, "How was your first day?" etc., etc. I said it was fine. I didn't want to explain about Scorpus and his gang. It made me feel embarrassed, even though it wasn't my fault.

I was seriously worried about going back to school the next day. Mrs. Protheroe had gotten us together with Scorpus and made him give my stuff back, which he did, with his face fixed in a sneer. He said he was only messing around, and she said she hoped there would be no repetition of the incident or Scorpus would be in serious trouble.

So that might sound all right, but outside the classroom, Scorpus had looked at us and said in a low, fierce voice like he was a bad guy in a soap opera, "I told you two losers if you told on me I'd kill you. And I *always* keep my word. See you after school."

Our last class was History with Miss Spiggins, which was close to the main entrance, so we were able to get out of school fast and run all the way home before Scorpus appeared. So, okay, that was a result. But we couldn't keep dodging him forever.

It turned out we'd picked the absolute worst person in the school to get on the wrong side of. Really. It was like making an enemy of Doctor Doom or Darth Vader or someone. Scorpus was a terror. A legend. He was the toughest kid in school, and last year he'd been suspended for assaulting a teacher. His dad was a well-known local thug. He'd just come out of prison after doing time for breaking a man's jaw in a bar and then breaking the nose of the cop who came to arrest him. So I didn't want my mom and dad going to the school to complain and have a meeting with Scorpus's parents so they could tell them off in their stuck-up voices using lots of long words. I had a feeling that wouldn't exactly help.

So when my dad got home from work that evening and asked me how it was, I told him it was fine, too.

"So they didn't eat you?" said Ben, scratching his head.

"No, not yet," I said.

My dad sat back in the armchair and sighed. "I'm glad your first day at school went well, Sam. Wish I could say the same about my day at work."

"Why?" my mom said. "They didn't . . . ?"

"They did," my dad said in this deep kind of gravelly voice he uses when he's being dead serious. "Roger Haggerston said the restructuring is going to take place next month. And my department is . . . vulnerable."

Mom looked stricken. Money's always been a little tight in our house. Not as tight as in Evan's, but still. Tightish. We're not one of those families that has a giant high-definition TV or buys a new car every year or goes on fancy vacations.

"What do you mean, 'vulnerable'?"

"I mean vulnerable—you know what that means, don't you?"

Maeve stuck her head around the living room door. She was just about to go out with her friends—she was wearing a short skirt and a tight top and about two pounds of makeup, but she still looked incredibly bad-tempered. "What? What's vulnerable?"

"My job."

"What do you mean, Dad? They're *firing* you?"

"It's not definite yet."

"Oh great, that's *all* I need," Maeve said, and flounced out, banging the front door behind her.

"I'll punch Roger Haggerston's face in!" Ben said. He's only six, and it often looks like he's in a world of his own, but he picks everything up.

My mom was like, "What are we going to *do*?"

"I don't know," my dad said heavily. "If worst comes to worst, there'll be some severance pay, but I don't know how much."

"How can they do this to you after sixteen years?"

"They can do what they want."

He sounded so sad and tired that even the dog noticed, went up to my dad, and stuck his head on his knee. Dad stroked the dog's ears.

"Come on, Billiam. Should I take you for a walk?"

Billiam started leaping and running around. My dad got up and went to get the leash.

"I'll come," I said.

I just felt like getting out of the house. And maybe cheering my dad up a little.

It turned out to be a good thing that I went.

It was just getting dark. Me and Dad walked along, not saying much. I was thinking about having to go to school tomorrow and I suppose Dad was thinking about not having a job to go to anymore. But it was kind of comforting, somehow, to walk along together in silence.

A few streets from our house there's a small park where you can let dogs off the leash. Billiam ran backward and forward, looking for a stick. He found one and dropped it at my feet. I threw it and he galloped off after it.

"So," said Dad, "tell me a little more about school."

"It was all right."

"What classes did you have?"

"Oh, you know. English and stuff. The usual."

"You're Mr. Communicative, aren't you? Did you make any new friends?"

"Well, not yet, I just went around with Evan."

"But do they seem nice there? It's a good atmosphere?"

"Oh yeah, yeah. Very good. Yeah."

I'd already decided I wasn't going to lay the Scorpus problem on him, but after hearing about him probably losing his job I wasn't going to even more. I didn't want to add to his worries.

Billiam came bounding back with the stick. I threw it again and he galloped off after it again.

Dad pointed upward. "Look!"

A bright silver streak was moving across the velvety blue sky.

"Is that a shooting star?"

"That's right."

"Can you make a wish on it?"

Dad laughed. "Well, that's the story. It's really just a meteor, burning up as it hits Earth's atmosphere. A chunk of rock from space. So I don't quite see how it could grant wishes . . ."

"Well, I'm going to wish," I said. "You never know!"

"Better hurry before it burns up!"

My mind started working fast. As fast as the meteor. I could wish that Scorpus would leave me and Evan alone. Or that I was so strong, I could pick him up and toss him over the school wall. But then, what about Dad and his job—maybe I should wish he'd keep it? Or even get a promotion? And then I thought, if I wished for a million pounds it wouldn't matter about his job. And it was *then* I thought, *What if I wished for a million wishes? Then I could take care of everything.*

I want to make it clear that I didn't actually *believe* in the wish at this point. I didn't really think a piece of hurtling space-rock could or would change the world for me. It was just comforting to think about it—like it's sort of comforting to pray sometimes, even if you don't believe in God.

So I said, in my head, *I wish for a million wishes.*

The shooting star disappeared behind the trees.

My dad's like, "Did you wish?"

"Yeah, I wished."

"What for?"

"Better not tell. Or it won't come true."

My dad gave a little smile. A sort of slightly weary, grown-up smile. "I don't think it'll come true anyway, Sam."

"No, I guess it won't."

But in my head I was saying, *I wish Scorpus doesn't beat me or Evan up tomorrow. And I wish Dad keeps his job.*

Which meant, theoretically, I had nine hundred and ninety-nine thousand nine hundred and ninety-eight wishes left.

I didn't bother to wish for the million pounds, though. That seemed a bit *too* unlikely.

We turned back and walked home, and I went to bed.

* * *

The alarm clock went off like a bomb, bursting through an uneasy dream I'd been having about running through the school halls, being chased by Scorpus, and I kept slamming doors behind me, hoping to get at least two closed doors between me and him, but every time he flung open the previous door before I could shut the next one, if you see what I mean.

In books and movies, people always sit bolt upright in bed when they awake from a bad dream, but of course no one ever does that in real life. What you do is what I did—just lie there, feeling relieved it was only a dream, waiting for your heartbeat to slow down. Except in this case, I realized, there wasn't much to feel relieved about. The reality was as bad as the dream.

"Sam! Are you up yet?"

My mom's voice came floating up the stairs.

The clock said seven thirty. There was a parallelogram-shaped patch of sunlight on the wall at the end of my bed.

"Sam! Time to get up!"

I wish it was an hour earlier, I thought.

And that's when things got seriously weird.

My mom's voice stopped instantly. The clock said six thirty. And the patch of sunlight wasn't at the end of my bed, but at the corner of the room. And it wasn't a parallelogram anymore. It was more like a rhombus.

This time I *did* sit up. Not bolt upright, but I struggled into a sitting position and clutched my head. Maybe I was still dreaming? But it didn't feel like it. Everything felt *real*. I felt the softness of the quilt and the mattress shifting under me, heard birds singing outside and a car driving past in the distance.

This wasn't possible.

Was it?

"I wish I had . . . a cup of tea," I said.

And a nanosecond later, there it was, gently steaming on my bedside table. In my favorite mug, too, a blue one that I call Bluey. (Yeah, very original, I know.) I took a sip. It was perfect. Just strong enough, with the right amount of milk, and one (level) spoonful of sugar.

It was so weird, I wanted to burst out laughing. Could I get *anything* I wished for?

I wish I had scrambled eggs and toast, with bacon and a glass of orange juice. On a tray.

And the tray materialized, neatly balanced on my lap.

The food smelled delicious. I took a few mouthfuls, and it tasted delicious, too. But I was too excited to finish it. I wanted to try out more wishes.

I wish I had a million pounds!

The whole lower end of my bed dipped, and I was bounced upward, like on a seesaw, as a great big block of twenty-pound bills landed on it. It was about the size of a really big suitcase. *So that's what a million pounds looks like*, I thought.

I reached out and took one of the bills. It was brand-new, as flat and crisp as if someone had ironed it. And I could have as many of these as I wanted . . .

But I'd have to be careful. Because the wishes came true as soon as I thought them. And thoughts are so difficult to control. They just pop into your head. As soon as you decide not to think something, you're already thinking it. So if I just happened to think, I don't know, *I wish there was a tiger in the room . . .*

No!

Too late.

There it was.

A huge orange-and-black beast filling the space between my bed and the door, filling the room with its hot, wild, heavy, dangerous big-cat smell. The floorboards creaked and strained under its weight. Its great big furry yellow-eyed face stared into mine. It looked startled, obviously wondering what had happened—one second it was hunting in the jungle in India or somewhere and the next it was in this little carpeted room on the first floor of a house in England. It swished its tail. It growled.

I could *feel* its strength—it could knock my head off with one swipe of a paw.

"I wish you were gone!" I said as fast as I could.

Blip.

Gone. Only the smell lingered.

So I wished for that to go, too. And it did.

But I still had a problem. Any moment now another crazy thought could come into my head—like . . . *I wish*—

No, I don't—

I don't wish—

I wish the—

No, no, no, la-la-la-la, I don't wish that at all, no, let's think of something else—

I wish the world—

No, no, focus on something else, like if the Incredible Hulk and the Mighty Thor had a fight, who'd—

I wish the world would—

No I don't stop stop stop no—

I wish the world would e—

No I don't—I—

—and I suddenly shouted, "I wish my wishes would only come true when I say them aloud!"

I breathed out a long, shaky breath.

I'd come within a microsecond of wishing the world would end.

But now I was safe. I wasn't going to wish for anything stupid *aloud*, was I? To calm my jangled nerves, I wished for a little tiny orchestra to appear on top of the million-pound pile of twenties and play me some soothing music. And they appeared immediately, musicians the size of Action Men and Barbie dolls, the men in black suits, the women in long gowns, and the conductor in tails and a white bow tie, and they started tuning up.

And I lay back, thinking of all the things I could wish for but not doing anything about it yet, just luxuriating in the possibilities like a bubble bath. All my life, you see, ever since I was a really little kid, I've always wanted something magical to happen. When Mom used to read me stories about witches and elves and unicorns and stuff, or the Narnia books, or later, when I read the Harry Potter books for myself, I used to think what a pity it was, what a shame, that none of that magic stuff was actually *true*. That life just went on in the same old boring way, with Earth spinning around at a fixed rate and gravity doing its job 24-7, and nobody could fly or go invisible or transmogrify. But *now*—now *anything* was possible. The miniature orchestra played a beautiful miniature melody, all tiny and tinkly like it came out of a music box, and I lay there thinking of being able to make myself as small as them, or as big as a mountain, or to be able to breathe underwater and swim as fast as a shark, or travel to outer space on a rocket-powered bicycle . . . I couldn't stop grinning.

At seven thirty the alarm went off again. The parallelogram of sunlight was back on the wall at the end of my bed. I wished the musicians would go back to wherever they came from, and I wished the million pounds was stashed in the suitcase on top of my wardrobe.

And then my mom shouted up the stairs. "Sam! Time to get up!"

I gazed at my face in the bathroom mirror as I was brushing my teeth. I looked surprisingly normal. My eyes were bright and I kept smiling, but apart from that, you'd have said this was the face of an ordinary eleven-year-old boy with red hair and a few freckles. Not someone who could have anything in the world he wanted just by asking for it. And then I thought, *This is* true, *isn't it? I'm not just dreaming or insane?*

I wanted to ask the meteor, or whatever it was, that had given me the wishes. And then I realized I could make that happen any time I wanted.

"I wish . . ." I began, and then stopped. I was about to wish for the Wish-Answerer to appear, but I realized I didn't know how big meteors were. It might be too big to fit in the bathroom. It might be bigger than the house.

"I wish that you'd make yourself small, Mr. Wish-Answerer, and come here so I can ask you a few questions."

A chunk of rock, about the size of my head, materialized on the bathroom shelf in front of me. It was a sort of dark gray with reddish patches. Black smoke rose from it. I could feel the heat it gave out. It had two little thin legs and two little thin arms like twigs, and it had a sort of face that looked like it was made out of marks and bumps in the rock. It had a couple of dark hollows for eyes and a sticking-out thing in the middle that looked like a beak, and there was a sort of gash or fissure for its mouth.

"Er . . . pleased to meet you," I said.

That was a totally stupid thing to say, I know, but I was in a state of shock.

The Meteor didn't say anything but bent its skinny legs to make a little bow.

"So—who are you?"

The Meteor still didn't say anything but spread its skinny arms and gave a little shrug.

"Okay, I *wish* you'd tell me who you are."

I'm afraid there is no intelligible answer I could give you, the Meteor said. It had a serious, precise voice like a news anchor. Its mouth didn't move, though. *My name would take seven weeks to utter and would leave you none the wiser.*

"But can you tell me—this is all true, isn't it? I'm not crazy or dreaming?"

You are not crazy and you are not dreaming, the Meteor confirmed.

"So—you've given me a million wishes, right? And I can really have anything I want?"

As long as it is logically possible.

"What do you mean?"

I cannot grant wishes that do not make logical sense. If you wished for a round square, for example, that wish could not be granted.

Because no square by definition could ever be round.

Well, that was okay. I didn't want a round square anyway. The last thing I needed.

"Apart from things like that, though—whatever I wish for, I get? And there are no catches?"

Catches?

"Well, I mean, do I have to use the wishes wisely or something? Or do I have to wish for only good things?"

It's none of my business, the Meteor said. *Wish for whatever you like.*

I looked at the Meteor's little rocky face and it looked back at me. It sounds crazy, I know, but I couldn't think of any more questions to ask.

"Well, I suppose you can go back into space now."

Thank you, I will.

"Wait—if there's anything else I need to know, can I just wish for you to come back?"

You do not need to summon me. If you wish to know something, I will answer.

"Okay," I said. "Well . . . bye."

The next instant, there was nothing on the bathroom shelf except a glass full of toothbrushes, Dad's razor and can of shaving foam, Mom's aloe vera shower gel, and about a hundred little jars and tubes of stuff that Maeve rubbed in or squirted onto various parts of her body.

Walking to school with Evan. It was a mild morning, warm and bright. The trees still had all their leaves, but they were just beginning to be tinged with yellow. I felt happier and more alive than I'd ever felt in my life.

I could turn the sky green if I wanted, I thought. *I could make the lampposts dance.*

"What are we gonna do?" said Evan. "About Scorpus."

"Don't worry, I'll straighten him out."

"What? How are you gonna do that?"

"I haven't decided yet."

"Oh, that's great!" said Evan. "He hasn't decided yet! Well, let me know when you come up with a plan, won't you? It is, you know, like slightly kind of urgent."

"Don't worry." And then I started whistling, which must've been kind of annoying, I know, especially because I can't really whistle.

Evan's like, "Stop that horrible noise."

He had a point. It was a bit tuneless and breathy, and I couldn't hit the high notes properly. Or the low ones, either, really. So I said, "I wish I could whistle really well," and the next second a beautiful, rich melody came flowing out of me as if I was a blackbird or something. It was the same tune the mini-orchestra had played. Dunno what it was, but it was nice.

Evan stared at me. "You're weird this morning."

"Am I? I tell you what, Evan, do you wish your uniform fit you better?"

"Look, don't start—"

" 'Cause I do. I wish it fit you perfectly."

Evan's uniform moved on his body like it was a living thing. The sleeves flowed down to his wrists, the trouser legs flowed down to his ankles, and the jacket widened just the right amount.

Evan's mouth widened, too. It looked like a tunnel.

"How—how did . . . ?"

"Magic."

"No, but really—how?"

"Magic."

"But what did you *do*?"

"Magic."

That was all I'd answer the rest of the way to school. I guess it must have been kind of annoying.

Chapter Three

All morning I was waiting for Scorpus to make his move, but somehow or other our paths didn't seem to cross. Obviously, I could've just wished he'd come and find me, but I didn't quite want to do that. It didn't seem *sportsmanlike*, somehow, if you know what I mean. I wanted it to happen, like, naturally.

Anyway, the morning's lessons were fun, because they were so easy. Like in French— I'd never studied French before, except for learning "Frère Jacques" in primary school, but I wished I spoke it perfectly and astonished Miss Gravely by asking her, in perfect French, where she'd spent her summer holiday, and if she'd enjoyed it, and was it the first time she'd been to Greece, and what did she think of the economic situation there, and did she agree that very hot weather was nice provided it wasn't too humid? Evan and the whole class just sort of goggled at me.

"How did you learn to speak French like that?" Evan said.

"Magic."

It wasn't till lunchtime that Scorpus tracked us down. I was in the locker room with Evan, playing Wild Animals Top Trumps, but it wasn't much of a contest because I'd wished

I knew what all his cards were. I'd just beaten his alligator (20 mph) with my hare (45 mph) when Vanida Mookjai came running in and squealed, "Quick! Run! Scorpus is on his way!"

"Oh good," I said. "I've been wondering when he'd show up."

"Let's get out of here!" said Evan.

"If you leave now," I said, "you'll miss all the fun."

Anyway, there wasn't time to go anywhere, because the next moment Scorpus came and stood in the doorway of the locker room, with his long shadow streaming ahead of him, all the way to the tips of my toes. Two of his friends stood behind him. And there were more kids crowding behind them, eager to see the entertainment.

"Farter! Toilet brush! You're dead."

I just laughed.

As Scorpus walked toward me, I muttered under my breath, "I wish I was as strong as the Incredible Hulk, I mean as strong as he would be if he existed in real life."

Immediately, I felt a kind of awesome power flood my body. Like when you get an adrenaline rush but twenty times more powerful. I felt like a volcano waiting to blow.

Scorpus reached out to grab me.

I smashed my fist into his body as hard as I could. I have to say the result wasn't *exactly* what I'd expected.

In the comics or the movies, when the Hulk hits someone they might get knocked through a wall or sent flying into the distance. But they always get up again. They don't have to go to the hospital, they don't have broken bones, they don't *bleed*. But then, the Hulk normally hits enemies who have superpowers themselves. Or special armor or something.

This was different.

As my fist crashed into Scorpus's body there was a horrible splintering noise. He was catapulted backward and hit the wall with a thud, and he slid down so he was sitting on the floor with his head hanging onto his chest in a kind of grotesque manner. He couldn't seem to breathe—he was sort of heaving and moaning. Then he keeled over sideways and lay on the floor, completely still.

Oh terrific.

There was a horrified hush and then everyone who was watching started babbling at once.

"My God!"

"Oh my *God*!"

"Did you see that?"

"He just—"

"*Oh* my *God*!"

"Never seen anything like it!"

"Is he dead?"

"What did you *do*, man?" said Evan.

"I don't know." Then, under my breath, I said, "I wish I knew what's wrong with Scorpus."

And the solemn news anchor's voice of the Meteor, inside my head, went: *He has a fractured sternum, seven cracked ribs, and a punctured lung.*

Oh.

Right.

Just a *bit* more severe than I'd intended.

"Okay," I said quietly, "I wish Scorpus didn't have a fractured sternum and cracked ribs and a punctured lung. I wish he'd stop bleeding. I wish he'd get up."

Scorpus sort of hauled himself to his feet. He stood there in a kind of tottery way, and what with his pale face and the blood still trickling down his chin he looked like a zombie in a horror movie.

I put on this cold, hard voice like a teacher telling someone off—like Mrs. Protheroe should have told Scorpus off, but she wasn't really strict enough. "Scorpus, if there is any repetition of your thuggish behavior you'll be in serious trouble. You'll wish you'd never been born, Scorpus. I'll come down on you like a ton of bricks." (That was one of my dad's expressions.) "Do you get me?"

Scorpus just stared at me in what you might call a dazed manner.

"I *said*, do you *get* me?"

Scorpus slowly nodded.

"Then I suggest you go away and think very hard about what you've done and what it's led to. I think there are some lessons there for you, if you think about it very carefully."

Scorpus staggered away. The crowd parted to let him through.

I suddenly realized I was drenched in sweat. And my heart was hammering away like, well, like a hammer. In the hands of a demented hammerer.

I wished I wasn't as strong as the Hulk anymore, in case I hurt someone by accident.

But I felt good. Oh man, I felt . . . amazing.

Chapter Four

Walking home with Evan.

"All right," Evan demanded. "What's happening?"

"What do you mean?"

"You know what I mean! Are you really . . . *magic*?"

I thought about this. "Yeah, I suppose you could say that."

"But—*how* . . . ?"

"I wished upon this shooting star, I wished for a million wishes, and—"

"Wait a minute," Evan said. "That's not possible. A shooting star is just—"

"I know, it's just a meteor. A chunk of space-rock."

"So how can it grant wishes?"

"I dunno. It just did, that's all."

"But . . ." Evan got quiet and a sort of lost-in-thought look appeared on his face. He has this look sometimes. It's like he's gazing off into the remote distance trying to make out something no one else can see, and he ignores everything else.

"What?"

"Can you prove it?"

"What do you want me to do?"

"Wish for . . . ice cream."

To be honest, I was a bit disappointed in Evan. I thought he might have come up with something more interesting than that. But then he is kind of a greedy pig, so it's not that surprising I suppose.

"Sure thing. What flavor?"

"Vanilla and chocolate. Double scoop."

"Cone or cup?"

"Cone."

"Do you want anything on it?"

"Er, yeah, nuts and chocolate sauce."

"Did you get all that, Wish-Answerer? I wish for a double scoop of vanilla and chocolate ice cream, in a cone, with nuts and chocolate sauce. Actually, make it two." I wanted one myself.

The two ice cream cones materialized, one in each of my hands, so suddenly, it made me jump. I offered one to Evan.

Evan took it warily and peered at it as if it might hold some kind of explanation.

I licked mine. It was nice. "Go on, try it."

Evan licked his. "It's . . . *real*. It's . . .
delicious."

"Oh yes, you only get good stuff with my
wishes."

"But—I just don't get where they came
from. Stuff can't appear out of nothing!"

"It can with my wishes."

"But—*how*?"

"It's no good asking how, that's just the
way they work. It's like—the laws of the universe. Gravity. That just works, doesn't it, and
no one knows how?"

"But that's my point! You've just *broken*
the laws of the universe. You can't make ice
cream and chocolate and nuts out of . . . *air*.
Things just work in a certain way, they always
have. One element doesn't change into another,
just 'cause someone says they wish it would!
Gravity always operates in the same way.
Water never flows uphill. Light always travels

at the same speed. All that stuff. Those laws never change."

"Never up until *now*," I said. "But things are different now that I've got my wishes!"

Evan put on his lost-in-thought look again. "Look, if you're saying that you can just change the laws of physics whenever you like . . . that's kind of . . . hard to accept. Without a *lot* of evidence. Could you do, like, an experiment to prove it?"

"Sure thing. Like what?"

"Well then—*can* you make water flow uphill?"

"Easy-peasy lemon-squeezy!" I said. "I wish for a bottle of water." It appeared in my hand. "Now, watch this."

The street where we were standing was on a hill—not a steep one, but enough so that if you rode a bike up it, it was harder work than you expected—I knew from experience.

I spilled the water on the ground, and of course it immediately started to run down the hill, following all the little cracks in the sidewalk.

"I wish you'd start running uphill, water!" I told it.

The water collected itself and then started to crawl uphill, like a glistening, silvery snake. We watched it get smaller and smaller as it crawled away from us.

Then Evan looked at me.

I looked at Evan.

And we both burst out laughing.

There didn't seem to be anything else to do.

When we stopped laughing, I said, "What should we wish for now? Anything you like, just tell me."

Evan looked thoughtful again. He looked as if he was about to speak, then stopped.

"What?"

"No, nothing, I'll leave it to you. They're your wishes. You choose."

He looked at me expectantly, and I got a feeling there was something he wanted me to say, but I had no idea what it was.

"I tell you what," I said. "You were talking yesterday about *Gulliver's Travels*. Wouldn't it be fun to go really giant, so everyone was tiny . . . ?"

"Er, yeah," Evan said. Then he seemed to get more interested in the idea. "Yeah, that would be really great!"

"Let's do it!" I said. A strange excitement started to prickle in my belly. "We'd better go somewhere with a little more space, though. Otherwise we'll be tripping over houses and stepping on cars and stuff."

"We could walk up to the Common."

"Walk?" I said. "No need to bother with *that*!" And it occurred to me then that I wouldn't need to walk anywhere ever again if I didn't want to. Not that I've got anything against walking, in fact sometimes I really like it, but it's a bit, you know, time-consuming. "I wish we were up at the Common."

So the next instant there we were. The sudden change took my breath away. Green space all around us. A pleasant breeze blowing. There were a few dog walkers, and on the far side some little kids and their parents in the playground, and about a hundred yards away some boys were kicking a soccer ball around. They were going to get the shock of their lives in a minute, I thought.

"How big do you want to go?" I said.

"I dunno—about twenty yards high?"

"Sounds about right to start with. 'Course, we can always go bigger if we want to."

" 'Course we can."

My heart was pumping away like crazy and my stomach was doing cartwheels. I couldn't quite believe what we were about to do.

"Ready?"

"Ready."

"We'd better stand a little farther apart," I said. "Otherwise, when we start to grow we'll bump into each other."

"Oh yeah." He moved off, about fifteen yards away.

"Ready?"

"Wait—I just thought of something. You better wish our clothes grow, too, or we'll burst out of them and be naked. And that'll be embarrassing."

"Okay. I wish me and Evan were giants, sixty feet high, and our clothes still fit us, and we were all in the same proportions as now." I didn't want to be like a big, long, skinny piece of string, I wanted to be an actual giant, like in fairy tales.

And so . . . we started to grow.

It was the weirdest feeling. I could see the ground getting farther and farther away, as if I was going up in an elevator or a cable car, but at the same time I could feel the ground sort of expanding under the soles of my growing feet. And I could see Evan swelling up beside me, an idiotic grin of excitement on his face. We were inflating like a couple of giant balloons.

Only—this was the weirdest thing of all— we weren't getting lighter, like a balloon would as it filled up with air. We were getting *heavier*. I could feel my head drooping on my neck, like my neck was too weak to hold it up properly. And my body was getting so massive my legs couldn't support it properly. Even though my legs were growing, too, they weren't up to the job of keeping me upright—I was just *too* heavy. They started to buckle; I could feel them giving at the knees. I tried to wave my arms to help me keep my balance, but they were almost too heavy to move. It was like trying to wave tree trunks around.

I was going to fall, and I knew that falling from this height, at this weight, would be serious. I mean, *really* serious.

I mean, like, fatal.

I saw my own expression of panic mirrored on Evan's face as he tottered helplessly around.

"Quick!" His voice had gone deep and booming. "Wish we were lighter than air, or we're goners!"

"I wish we were lighter than air!"

Oh, the relief! The sweet merciful life-saving relief as I floated up off the ground! The horrible weight of my head that felt like it was going to break my neck was gone, my limbs were light and free, and the ground was no longer a terrifying enemy that was about to kill me, but a nice wide stretch of green grass that looked peaceful and friendly as I gradually rose above it.

The people on the Common were all pointing up and staring, shouting and jabbering, unable to believe their eyes.

"Whew!" Evan said. He was hovering just a few yards away. "That was close!"

"What happened?" I couldn't figure it out. "Why did we get so heavy? I didn't wish for that!"

Evan's like, "I should have thought of it. Of course when you get bigger you get heavier!"

"Yeah, obviously, but I still don't get it. If we're bigger all over—"

"That's the problem. The thing is, we got bigger in three dimensions. So we're over ten times *taller* than before, but more than a thousand times *heavier*."

"But what about dinosaurs? They were giant, and they could walk around okay."

"Yeah, but they'd evolved to be like that. Their skeletons were built to hold their weight. We're not the right *shape* to be so big; we weren't designed for it."

All this time we'd been drifting upward. Already the ground was far away. The Common now looked like a green spot in the middle of a big gray town. People looked like ants and cars were like little beetles. And it was getting cold. Like, really cold.

"It's freezing!" My teeth were chattering. And you can imagine the racket that made, when each tooth was about the size of an iPad.

"We're gonna keep rising 'cause we're lighter than air!" Evan's teeth were going like a set of giant castanets as well. "And it's gonna get colder and colder, and soon we won't be able to breathe. You have to do something!"

"Okay, okay, I get it!" I thought for a second. "I wish we were heavier than air, but only a little heavier. I want us to be able to walk around all right. And also I wish we don't step on anyone or squash anyone."

We started to sink pretty fast, but not scarily fast. It was like dangling from a parachute. Or that's what I'd guess, anyway, seeing as I've never done a parachute jump. The air got warmer again. My giant goose bumps disappeared.

The green grass came surging toward us. There were more people there now, hundreds of them, all around the edges of the Common, and there were cops trying to keep them back. They all had their phones out, taking pictures of us. A TV camera crew was just arriving, piling out of their vans and setting up equipment.

"I've always wanted to be on TV!" I said.

Evan grinned and was just saying "Me too!" when we landed. It made us stagger a little, and we both lurched toward the watching crowds. They screamed and started to stampede backward, falling over and stepping on each other. It was crazy.

Oh great, I thought. I said, "I wish no one gets hurt, and I wish no one was scared of us."

The crowd calmed down then. They regrouped and pressed nearer to us, craning their necks up and going "Wow!" "Ooh!" "Aah!" etc., etc., like people do when they're watching really amazing fireworks or something.

"What shall we do now?" I said.

"Go for a walk?" Evan suggested.

"Yeah, why not?"

So we walked off the Common and into the town. It was weird 'cause each step bounced us up in the air and then we came drifting down again. It was like walking on the moon.

The crowd followed us, and more people joined them as we bounced along through the streets. They were running out of their houses, pouring down the streets toward us from every direction.

It was funny seeing the town from this height. Houses came just past our knees, and even apartment buildings were only around head height. And I could see all the different streets and the way they were laid out—for the first time I really got the shape and pattern of the town I'd lived in all my life. It was sort of like when I went on vacation to the Isle of Wight when I was eight, and we went to this place, Godshill, where they had a model village you could walk around. But this was a model village with real, tiny people in it, running after us, or waving at us from top-floor windows.

✱ ✱ ✱

Well, you might think you'd never get bored of being a giant and walking around being followed by cheering crowds and filmed by TV crews (a couple of helicopters had turned up and they had cameras going, too). But the truth is, once we'd walked around town a couple of times the novelty started to wear off. I mean, it was still great, but I started to think, *What next?*

"What next?" Evan said.

"I dunno. Do you want to go even bigger?"

"I dunno."

I heard a tiny voice squeaking, "Sam! Sam!" and I looked down and there was Maeve with three of her friends, on the High Street.

I bent down. "Hiya, Maeve."

"Sam! What's happened?" Her eyes were bright with amazement, and she was grinning her head off. I realized it was the first time I'd seen her so excited or interested in anything for ages. She'd been in a bad mood ever since her boyfriend, Stefan Bumgarner, dumped her. (That's not a joke, by the way. He really is called that.) He'd started going out with another girl who Maeve really hates, Josephine Waxwing. And she'd hardly smiled since. She must have been feeling pretty depressed, I suppose.

"How did you get so *big*?" she squealed.

"Growth spurt, I guess." I put my hand flat on the sidewalk in front of her. "Climb on, I'll show you the view from up here!"

They all scrambled up and squashed together on my hand—which to them was about the size of a double bed. I slowly rose up, holding my hand as steady as I could. They were all screaming with laughter and clutching onto each other and sliding around.

It was when they were about ten yards up that the accident happened.

Loren stumbled and caught hold of Lola, who also stumbled, and they tripped over my thumb—so to save them I tilted my hand—but I tilted it too far and too quickly, and Maeve and Miriam slid off the other side and went plummeting down, screaming their heads off.

I made a desperate grab at them with my free hand, but missed. They hit the sidewalk with two sickening cracks, like a pair of eggs being dropped.

The crowd gasped.

"Whoops!" said Evan.

Maeve and Miriam lay sprawled out, limbs twisted, unmoving.

The helicopters swept down toward the bodies to get better pictures.

A feeling of guilt and dread filled me, as if I'd just smashed two priceless vases in a museum or something, only much, much worse because they weren't things, they were *people*, and one of them was my own sister. I'd only had the wishes a few hours and already I'd seriously injured or killed three people. I was like a one-man crime wave.

But I still had the wishes, didn't I? That was the great thing about having a million wishes (or nine hundred and ninety-nine thousand nine hundred and whatever-it-was). Nothing was unchangeable. Consequences were optional.

"I wish they were alive again," I said. "And completely unhurt."

Maeve and Miriam got up, dusting themselves off. The crowd sighed with relief.

"Sam, you stupid idiot!" Maeve shouted up at me.

"Sorry, bit of a butterfingers there . . ." That's one of my mom's expressions. It seemed to fit.

"You could have killed us!"

"Yeah, well, I didn't."

I put the other two girls down beside Maeve and Miriam. Carefully.

One of the helicopters buzzed right in front of my head and I could see the cameraman training his camera on me, trying to get a good shot of my face. I had to fight off an urge to swat it away like a fly. Now the whole stupid episode of me dropping those girls would be on the news. It would be broadcast by TV stations all over the world and get a billion hits on YouTube . . .

I looked at Evan and he gave me a look with raised eyebrows and a downturned mouth, shrugging his shoulders, and I realized I was doing the same look myself, and the look meant, "What the heck are we doing here?" Suddenly, the idea of being on TV didn't seem so great, and stomping around the streets of town while being twenty yards tall didn't seem big or clever anymore. Well, it was big, obviously, but not clever.

I was like, "Let's get out of this."

Evan nodded his colossal head.

I was like, "I wish me and Evan were normal size again." And immediately, *so* immediately, it made me feel giddy, we were standing on the sidewalk together, normal size like everyone else, and trees and buildings we'd looked down on a moment ago now towered over us. "And I wish those helicopters would buzz off. I wish everyone would just forget seeing us as giants. I wish the film in all the camera crews' cameras turns out to be blank."

The crowd lost interest in what you might call an abrupt manner. They streamed off in different directions. Maeve and her friends went off toward the shopping mall without another glance at us.

"Now what?" Evan said.

"I dunno," I said. "Tell you what—we've tried being giants. How about being tiny next? Just like Gulliver. That'd be a laugh."

"Yeah, I suppose it would."

I'd always been fascinated by the idea of being really teeny-tiny, so that ordinary objects were giant-size—you know, like a pencil would be the size of a telegraph pole and a pea would be like a pumpkin and a caterpillar would be like a giant snake with legs.

But I didn't want to go small here on the High Street. I didn't want to draw attention to us again, which would definitely happen if we suddenly disappeared. Also, we might get stepped on. Better to do this one indoors, at least to start with.

"Let's go to my house first."

"All right." He turned to start walking off.

"What're you doing? Walking's a thing of the past, man!"

"Oh yeah. Right."

"I wish me and Evan were in my bedroom."

My bedroom walls appeared around us, and the bed materialized so suddenly behind me that I sat down on it.

Chapter Five

"How small do you wanna go?"

Evan considered this. "About five inches? For starters?"

"You got it. I wish we were five inches tall, and our clothes still fit!"

The room seemed to explode. The walls went rushing away and the ceiling zoomed upward. My wardrobe on the other side of the room suddenly looked as big as an apartment building. The bed I was sitting on turned into a gigantic area, about the size of a soccer field. A soft, bouncy soccer field.

Evan was on the carpet, looking up at me. The drop from my bed to the floor was about two feet, I guess, but at my current size that was the equivalent of about seven and a half yards. It made me feel dizzy.

"How do I get down from here?"

"Can't you climb?"

It was true that there was a bit of the quilt hanging over the edge. If I climbed down that and dangled from the end, I'd be near enough to the floor to be able to drop the last part of the way. Still, it looked pretty scary. If I slipped . . .

"Or you could just wish to be down here," Evan said.

Well, that was true, too. But I suddenly thought, what's the point of always wishing things were already done instead of doing them? Being tiny was an adventure, after all—I might as well make the most of it.

I grabbed the quilt and started to inch down. It was harder than I'd thought. Gripping a fistful of quilt is easy when you're full-size. But at five inches high, your hands are so small that they can't grab very much of it. It felt much coarser than normal, like stiff canvas.

I started to sweat. I glanced down and the floor still looked a long, long way away. If I fell I'd be all smashed up, like when Maeve fell off my hand earlier . . .

And then I felt my hands slipping.

I fell, leaving my stomach behind.

The wind rushed past my ears.

I heard Evan give a sort of squeak of alarm.

Too late, I started to shout "I wish—"

I hit the floor.

But I didn't hit it with a bang. It was more a sort of *ploomph*, plus a little bit of a rustle.

It didn't hurt at all. The carpet was deep and springy, coming up to my ankles.

"Are you all right?" Evan ran toward me over the springy carpet.

"Totally. It feels like I just fell, well, off a bed."

Evan laughed. "Of *course*! You *did* just fall off a bed. It looks a long way to us, but it's still only a short drop, really—and because we weigh so much less, you hit with much less force than usual. Do you realize what this means?"

"No—what?"

"We don't have to worry about gravity at all. At this size, it can't hurt us! Watch!"

He ran across the room and started trying to climb up the wardrobe, but it was too smooth and he kept slipping down.

"Wish I was on top of the wardrobe, Sam!"

"Okay, I wish you were on top of the wardrobe."

There he was, next to my suitcase full of money. I'd forgotten about that. He spread his arms like a diver and launched himself off into space.

I clutched my face in alarm—even though he'd said it was safe, it did still look like a horribly long drop . . .

He hit the carpet, rolled, and got up with a big grin all over his face.

"You try!"

So for the next five minutes we played at jumping off the wardrobe. It was amazing— like bungee jumping, I guess, but we didn't have to worry about hitting the ground. We were so light, we *couldn't* hurt ourselves.

"I bet we could jump from higher—I bet we could jump from the roof of the house!"

I was like, "D'you think?"

"'Course. Look, we only weigh about as much as mice—and if a mouse fell off the roof it would be okay, wouldn't it?"

"I dunno."

"Wish you knew, then."

"Oh yeah. I wish I knew if a mouse would hurt itself if it fell off the roof of our house."

And the little news anchor's voice in my head said, No. It would receive a slight shock and scamper away unharmed.

"I wish we were on the roof of our house, then!"

We sat on the ridge at the very top of the roof. Slate-gray tiles, each one about the size of our bathroom floor, sloped away from us. The yard was so far below, it looked like another country.

"This is it," Evan said. "The big one!"

I took a deep breath.

Evan stood up. "You ready?"

I nodded. I stood up.

I heard a beat of wings behind me, and a huge bird swooped down and snatched me up in its horrible, big, spiky talons, and flew off with me.

Chapter Six

The talons were gripping me tightly and it really hurt. I craned my neck around to look at the bird. It was like something out of a horror movie. When you see birds pecking on the lawn they can look really cute. But when you see them close up they're about as cute as a great white shark. This one had a cruel curved beak and blank, psychotic eyes. It was planning to eat me, and it wouldn't suffer a moment's remorse. Scientists say birds are descended from dinosaurs, and all I can say is, I believe it.

"I wish I was my normal size again!"

The bird gave a squawk of surprise. Its talons slipped off me. And I started to accelerate toward earth, which, now that I was normal-size again, was capable of killing me. I was also completely naked because I'd forgotten to wish my clothes would grow with me.

"I wish I was five inches again!" I got the wish out just before I hit the lawn. So I didn't do myself any serious damage, but it was an uncomfortable landing. Now that I was tiny again, each blade of grass was about thigh high and as thick as my hand. It also felt very hard and coarse—more like reeds than grass.

This was turning out to be a stressful day.

I wished for my clothes back. I also wished

that the bird would have a really bad headache for the rest of the day. A little spiteful, maybe. But after all, that was nothing compared to what it would've done to me.

Evan had watched all this from the roof, and then he jumped down beside me on the lawn.

"Wow, that was close!"

"Tell me about it."

"That was a sparrowhawk! They're quite rare around here, you know."

"They can't be too rare for me."

"But you have to admit, they're magnificent birds."

"What?"

"They're magnificent birds."

"You wouldn't say that if one had just carried you off."

"Yes I would."

"No you wouldn't."

"Yes I would."

"All right, then, let's see. I wish a sparrow-hawk would come along and carry Evan off."

Down it swooped. It carried Evan off, dangling from its talons. Evan's face featured three big circles—his round, astonished eyes and his round, gaping mouth.

It sounds mean, I know. It's just . . . when it's so easy to wish for something and you *know* it'll come true right away, you often find yourself wishing for stuff before you've really thought it through.

In no time, Evan was a speck in the distance. I wished the bird would bring him back unharmed and put him down on the ground beside me. So it came winging its way back, and as Evan came into focus I saw that now his face wasn't defined by three circles but by three straight lines. His eyes were narrowed and his lips were set in a line of anger.

"Do you still think it's a magnificent bird?" I asked him.

"Yes, it's magnificent. But you're not!" His face was flushed and he was panting slightly. "Look!" He pulled up his shirt to show big red marks where the talons had gripped him.

"All right, then, I wish those red marks were gone." At once, Evan's skin was back to its pale, unmarked, flabby normality. "Happy now?"

"Not really."

"Well, what else can I do?"

"You could try saying sorry."

Now, I don't know about you, but I hate being told to say I'm sorry. I'm happy to say it if I *feel* sorry, but as soon as someone orders me to say it, I stop feeling it. So I really didn't want to say it. But then, I didn't want Evan to keep feeling annoyed with me. So . . .

"I wish Evan didn't feel annoyed with me anymore."

"I don't," Evan said. He grinned. "I'm not annoyed with you at all."

"Well, that's all right, then. What should we do now?"

"I'm getting a little hungry," said Evan.

What a surprise.

Still. I suppose I was kind of hungry myself. "What should we have?"

"Burger and fries?"

"Coming right up. I wish for two Burger King Whoppers and fries . . ." Then my mind took a leap. "Giant-size!"

Wow.

I've always been fascinated by the idea of giant-size food. And there it was, steaming, smelling delicious, two boxed burgers, each one about the size of a van. And next to each one, a bag as high as my head, with golden fries poking out of it like planks of wood.

I pulled one of the fries out. I had to use both hands. It was too hot to hold for long, so I wished for it to cool down, just a little bit, and then I took a bite.

Hmm.

It wasn't *quite* as delicious as I'd thought. To begin with, the outside was a little leathery— of course, it was about fifteen times as thick as before, so it was very hard to bite into. Also, when you're not much bigger than the fry your-self, you notice just how greasy they are. That is, very greasy. And the fine dusting of salt they have? Well, when you're five inches tall, it's not a fine dusting at all but chunks of rock salt, each one about as big as a grain of rice. I took a few bites anyway, but soon got tired of it and put the fry down in the grass. So did Evan.

"Maybe the burgers will be better," Evan said.

It was hard to wrestle the boxes open, so I just wished they'd open up. We each climbed into a box. The burger came up to about my waist, and by leaning forward and spreading my arms I could just about touch both sides. I saw that Evan was tearing chunks out of the roll and then pulling out fistfuls of burger to put in them—effectively making mini-burgers, which turned out to be the only way we could eat them. Even then it wasn't easy. We couldn't eat the sesame seeds—they were much too big and hard, so we had to pull those out and throw them away. The sauce and mayo and stuff inside? Well, there was buckets of it, and it got all over my clothes, adding to the grease stains the fry had already left there. The lettuce was thick and fibrous, like giant raw cabbage leaves. And the meat was coarse and gristly and fatty.

It *was* fun, because it was so weird. But the burger wasn't particularly good to eat. Soon I felt sick and had to stop. Evan battled on for a little while, but eventually even he had to give up.

We lay on the grass—I wished for a miniaturized patch so it would be more comfortable—and sipped on micro-sized glasses of Coke (otherwise the bubbles would have been too big to swallow).

And I tried to figure out in my head what exactly having all these wishes meant and what I was going to do with them. I mean, so far, all I'd done was mess around. Was I going to continue doing that? Well, maybe. It was pretty spectacular messing around, after all. But . . . it might get boring. No, not even boring, that wasn't the right word.

More . . . *unsatisfying*. Like just *playing* at life instead of actually living it. Because when you can have whatever you want, without any effort at all—did anything actually mean anything?

"Sam?"

"Yeah?"

"You could wish for *anything*, couldn't you?"

"Looks that way."

"No limits?"

"I don't think so."

"Well . . . I wonder if . . . you could . . . ?"

"What?"

"I was just thinking . . ."

"What?"

"You know." He looked at me with a kind of hopeful, pleading expression.

"What?" Maybe you'll think it was pretty dumb of me, but I couldn't figure out what he was leading up to.

Just then, a distraction occurred. "Hey, look at that!" I said.

A line of ants was marching up the side of one of the burger boxes. And another line was heading for the discarded fry. But when I say ants, you have to realize that, from our perspective, these were really big, bad boys. Each one was roughly the size of a lobster.

"Oh my God!" said Evan. He wandered over to look at them more closely. So did I. They ignored us, just kept on filing past like robots. "They're kind of horrible, aren't they?" Evan said. "Like little monsters. Or aliens."

"I wonder what they'd look like if we were *really* small."

We looked at each other.

"I wish we were one millimeter tall!" I said, and the world changed.

The blades of grass were no longer reeds,

but trees. They towered over our heads, casting a green gloom. The soil under our feet wasn't smooth but rough and chunky, full of clods and pebbles. And the ants—the ants! They were as big as rhinos now. You could actually hear the swoosh of the grass they parted, and hear their feet—if ants have feet; you know what I mean, the ends of their legs— grating on the pebbles as they tramped past.

In *Honey, I Shrunk the Kids*, if you've seen that movie, the kids meet an ant in the backyard and make friends with it. It's a cute ant and it communicates with them by squeaking and twitching its antennae, and it lets them ride around on its back. I have to tell you that that movie is totally bogus. There's *nothing* cute about ants. They're hideously ugly. When you see them close up in supersize it's amazing how crude and unfinished they look, like they're bolted together out of spare parts.

They've got horrible, big, goggly eyes, which are completely empty of expression, and coarse hairs like steel wires sticking out of their legs, and great big mandibles dripping with some sort of horrible saliva. They've got a sort of pungent, acidic smell to them as well, like a mixture of sweat and vinegar. You can just tell, looking at them, that they have no soul, no intelligence whatsoever—they are just dumb machines blindly following a program. Creepy or what? I felt a sudden, senseless desire to kill them. Destroy them all.

"Shall we?" I went.

"What?"

"Blast them."

"But why?"

"It'll be fun."

"But it's killing for fun, isn't it? Like hunting. And I don't agree with hunting."

"Neither do I. But come on, Evan, these are *ants*! They haven't got any feelings. Look at them!"

"Well . . ."

I could see he was wavering. "I wish we each had a bazooka, just the right size for us to hold but powerful enough to blow up an ant!"

And there, in my hands, was this sort of steel tube with a trigger and a telescopic sight. I lifted it onto my shoulder and looked down the sight at the nearest ant. I aimed at its bulky, bulbous head and pressed the trigger.

Wham!

A stream of yellow fire shot out and hit the ant. It burst into flames and fell over, with its six legs jerking around randomly.

A second later, another streak of flame shot out from Evan's bazooka and another ant went up in flames and fell over.

The other ants took no notice. They just skirted around their fallen comrades and headed straight for the burgers. And I think it was this that convinced me that the ants deserved no mercy at all. They didn't even care about each other, so why should I?

I pumped the trigger again and again and again, and so did Evan, and the big, lumbering beasts collapsed, burst into pieces, writhing and kicking, with no idea what had hit them. I realized I was laughing, and so was Evan.

It had been a dry summer. The flames from the burning ants soon caught the surrounding grass. In no time, a forest fire had started. Me and Evan retreated, still firing, but the flames were roaring toward us. I felt the heat searing my face.

"Sam!" Evan shouted. "Do something!"

"I wish we were full-size!"

Darn! I'd forgotten about the clothes again. The doll-size outfits we'd worn lay torn and tattered on the grass, and we were both stark naked.

"All right, I wish we had our clothes on, obviously!"

We stood on the lawn, with the little ring of fire flickering at our feet. The ants were running around in circles, tiny, confused black specks—the burger attracted them while the flames drove them away.

I suddenly felt sorry for them. The poor little things didn't know what they were doing, they just followed their instincts. I started to stamp out the flames, and so did Evan. I tried to avoid stamping on any ants. But that was impossible, of course.

When the fire was out, I felt a little silly and ashamed of myself. What had we just been doing? It was like we'd gone crazy.

"I wish all those ants we killed were alive again," I said.

Evan nodded in agreement. "What's the matter with us? With all those wishes—you could do anything in the world—and we're wasting our time killing *ants*!"

"I know."

"I mean, instead of killing things, we could . . ."

"What? Look, if there's something you want me to wish, why don't you just tell me?"

Evan bit his lip. "You mean you can't guess?"

"Nothing's coming to me."

"Well—think about it, okay?"

"Okay." He'd gone all serious. I couldn't figure out why he was acting so weird.

"I'm gonna go home now," Evan said.

"Okay. See you tomorrow."

At the gate he turned back. "Just one more thing . . ."

"Yeah?"

"Could you wish for a burger for me to eat on the way home? A normal-size one?"

"Sure," I said. "Was that it—the thing you wanted me to guess?"

"No," Evan said. "That wasn't it."

Chapter Seven

I could tell by the way Dad came home that evening that he was in a good mood. He flung the door open and bounced into the hall. He was carrying a bottle of wine in one hand and a bunch of flowers in the other. And his face looked . . . bright. Happy. Young.

Mom came out into the hall. He handed her the flowers and gave her a kiss.

"What's with the flowers? What have you done?"

"I've kept my job!"

"What? How come?"

"I don't know. Roger Haggerston came into my office today and told me my job was guaranteed!"

"So they're not restructuring?"

"I don't know. But if they do, my job won't be affected!"

"That's great news, Dad!" I said.

Maeve appeared at the top of the stairs. She'd just gotten out of the bath, and she was in a dressing gown with a towel wrapped around her head. "What? You're not getting fired?"

"No, Maeve. I'm not getting fired."

"That's something, I suppose." She disappeared back into her room.

"But are you sure you can trust them?" Mom said suspiciously. She's found it hard to trust anyone since things all went wrong with her own job. She used to be the manager of an

art shop. But she left because she wanted to be
an artist herself. She spent every day painting
in the shed at the end of the yard. But she never
sold a single painting, even though the shop
she used to manage let her put on an exhibition there. Then she tried to get her old job
back but the owner had given it to someone else.

"Oh, I think so. Roger sounded like he
meant it."

"You might even get a promotion, Dad!"
I said.

Dad laughed. "Well, you never know."

"That's right," I said. "You never know!"

"We should have a special dinner to cele-
brate!" Dad said.

Mom looked doubtful. "Just because
you've kept your job—for the time being—
doesn't mean we have to spend your salary all
at once. We still have to budget, you know."

"Well, I know, but . . ."

I went into the kitchen, where no one could hear me, and made a few quick wishes.

A few moments later, there was a knock at the door. I went back into the hall to watch Mom open it. There was a delivery man standing there with two great big bags. A delicious smell of Chinese food wafted into the house.

"Madam, I am from Jade Garden, the new gourmet Chinese restaurant, the finest in the area. As a special promotion we are bringing you, honored customers chosen at random, the special Emperor's Banquet, entirely free of charge. Enjoy!"

He left the bags on the doorstep, got on his moped, and zoomed off into the twilight.

Dad poked his nose into the bags and peeled back the lid of one of the plastic containers. The smell of delicious food intensified.

"Is it some sort of joke?" my mom said.

"I don't think so," Dad said. "At least, the food seems real enough!"

Ben ran in from the living room. "Is that Chinese food?"

"Yeah," I said, "it's the Emperor's Banquet."

"My flavorite!" said Ben. He said that by mistake a few years ago and everyone laughed, so he continued saying it. We don't laugh anymore—we're actually a little fed up with it.

"Let's set the table and open the wine!" my dad said. "This is turning out to be a strange day. But a good one! I wonder what'll happen next."

"I expect there'll be an earthquake and the house will fall down a chasm," said my mom. "Or we'll all be trapped in a fire." She likes to bring things back down to earth.

"No, I think some other good stuff might happen," I said. "It's just a feeling I've got."

While we were eating (it was the most delicious Chinese food any of us had ever eaten—I'd wished that it would be), the phone rang. Mom went to get it. We could hear her going, "What? . . . Who is this? . . . Yes . . . But . . . Is this for real? . . . I can't quite believe this is happening, but . . ." Then she burst out laughing—not the sort of laugh when something's funny, but the sort of laugh when you're so happy you can't stop yourself. "Of course! I'd be delighted! Yes . . . tomorrow . . . See you then. I can't wait!"

She came back to the table. Her face was pink and dazed with delight.

"What is it, Mom?" Maeve asked.

"That was Bernard Souter, the London art critic! He said . . . he said he slipped into my exhibition incognito last year—and it was the best new work he's ever seen! He wants to come and have another look at the paintings tomorrow—he wants to buy some—and he's been working very hard to organize a major exhibition for me at the Tate Modern and they've finally agreed—it's going to be next month!"

"That's fantastic, darling!" my dad said.

"He said all that conceptual stuff—sharks in tanks and all that—everyone's fed up with that now. They want good old-fashioned paintings like mine, executed with skill and technique!"

Maeve's like, "You sure it's not a trick? Someone imitating Bernard Souter's voice?"

"Who's Bernard Spouter?" Ben asked, scratching his head. He's had lice ever since he started nursery school. And that was three years ago. He gets lice-combed every night but they always come back.

Some of the glee faded from Mom's face.

"Oh . . . I suppose it could be a hoax. But who would be cruel enough to do that?"

"People are horrible, Mom," Maeve said. "I thought that was a well-known fact."

"I bet it's not a hoax," I said.

"What's a hoax?" Ben asked, still scratching.

"You can't trust anyone," Maeve said. "No one. No one at all."

Her phone gave a little tinkly noise. She pulled it out to read the text. Her face went as dazed and pink as Mom's had just done.

"What is it?" Dad asked.

"It's from Stefan!"

"What? Bumgarner?" Dad said. He's never been able to get over Bumgarner's name. Well, none of us have, really.

"What's he say?" Mom asked. "Looks like good news."

"Yeah, it's . . . you could say that, yeah," Maeve said. But she didn't read the text out loud. She didn't need to, I knew what it said:

> Ive been thinking what an idiot ive
> been. u r the only girl 4 me ever,
> ive been so miserable since we split, I
> cant believe what a moron I was. u r
> the best girl in the world and I am just
> a stupid idiot. And Josephine is horri-
> ble and smelly. Would u take me back?
> Please? Even though I dont deserve it?
> Cos I luv u Maeve, I truly do.

"You sure it's not a hoax?" I asked.

But I was only teasing. It wasn't a hoax. For once, everyone was going to get what they wanted. And it felt good.

The next person to straighten out was Ben. Not that he had any real problems. You don't really when you're six, only those lice, but I thought I might as well get rid of them for him. Really destroy them. Eradicate them. Obliterate them once and for all.

After we'd eaten, and Maeve had gone upstairs to phone all her friends and Mom and Dad were in the kitchen, loading the dishwasher, I said, "I'll give Ben his bath and lice-comb him tonight."

"Oh, you don't have to do that, Sam," Mom said.

"Why not?" said Dad. "Let him do it. We can settle down on the sofa and finish the wine in front of the TV!"

✳ ✳ ✳

I sat on the toilet seat. Ben was in the bathtub, telling me a long story about what had happened in school that day. "Fatima said I shouldn't be in the top group for Math, so I asked her what seven and seven was and she said seventy-seven and I said don't be silly that's wrong and she said she was only joking so I said what's the real answer then and she said she knew but she wasn't going to say so I said it's fourteen actually and she said she knew that all along and then she went around telling everyone I didn't know what seven and seven was and I was just telling her off for saying lies about me and then Miss Martinez told me off for talking and that wasn't fair because she told *me* off but not Fatima and said if I kept talking I'd have to be moved out of the top Math group away from all my friends and Fatima's not even my friend!"

"Yeah, that's terrible." He's always going on about this Fatima girl. I think they like each other a little, that's why they're always egging each other on.

"If they take me out of the top Math group it's not fair. Then Fatima will laugh at me. She's already in the top Literacy group and I'm not."

"Listen, Ben, stay still. I'm gonna lice-comb you in a special way today."

"What're you gonna do?"

I hesitated a little. I hadn't been planning to tell him, but now I thought if I didn't, he'd wonder where I'd gone and call out for Mom and Dad. Also, he might scratch his head and squash me.

"Listen, Ben, don't be alarmed—"

"Like an alarm clock?"

"Yeah, don't be alarmed like an alarm clock. I'm gonna get tiny and go into your hair and hunt the lice down."

Now, of course, I didn't need to do this. I could have just wished the lice would vanish. But I wanted to make an adventure out of it. A quest. Otherwise, I thought, life would get too boring if I never had to actually *do* anything. Okay, the ant-killing hadn't been as much fun as I'd expected. But this was different. Lice had been driving Ben mad for three years. They deserved their comeuppance. And I was going to be the one to give it to them.

Ben looked at me in a kind of solemn way. "That's impossible."

"I know it is."

"If it's impossible, you can't do it."

"Yes I can, because I'm magic."

"If you're magic, turn into a helicopter."

"I'll *get* you a helicopter, if you just sit still and don't scratch your head, all right?"

"What color helicopter?"

"Any color."

"Can I have a helicopter that's got spots like a leopard?"

"Yeah, if you just sit still and don't scratch your head, all right?"

Ben nodded. "All right."

"In a second, I'm gonna get so small, you won't see me," I said. "But I wish you won't be scared, okay?"

"I won't be scared."

"No, you won't. All right, so I wish I was really small, about twice as big as a louse, and I wish I was in Ben's hair, and I wish I had a sharp, shining sword of just the right size!"

The next instant, I was in a brown forest, with big strands of hair as thick as my arm sprouting up all around me, droplets of water as big as coconuts clinging to them, and a forest floor of pink scalp.

I heard Ben's voice, loud and echoey in the tiled bathroom, commenting on the situation quite calmly. "Sam's gone. He's gotten small. He's in my hair. He's killing lice."

I made my way through the forest, following the pink paths through the giant hairs, looking all around, sword at the ready. I heard a kind of scritching noise and steered toward it. A moment later, I came face-to-face with my first louse.

Well, I'd thought ants were ugly. But compared to lice, the ants were movie stars. Beauty queens. Visions of loveliness.

The louse in front of me was around the size of a large dog. It had two wiggling antennae, six waving legs that ended in claws, and a fat tail like a fish. It looked like it was made out of some sort of semi-transparent jelly. You could see all the blood swirling around inside it. Its face—well, I don't know whether to call it a face, exactly—was soft and doughy, with a black oval eye on each side. Like something out of a nightmare. Its mouth parts were plugged into Sam's scalp and it was sucking greedily. You couldn't imagine a more repulsive creature. No one could like it. Even their own mothers don't like them. They just lay their eggs and crawl off to a different part of the head.

I walked right up to it. The stupid, dumb creature just kept on sucking.

"This is the end of the line for you, louse!" I said.

But I don't think it heard, because they don't have any ears. I plunged my shining sword into its side. A pale liquid gushed out, streaked with blood. The creature wriggled but kept on sucking. I cut its head off, and it finally stopped.

When I'd first thought of this scenario, I'd imagined that every time I killed one I'd throw it off Sam's head to land in the bathwater. But that wasn't possible. It was too big and I was too small and I'd never get it past the forest of hairs. I'd just have to let the corpses lie where they fell and comb them out after.

One down. Lots more to go.

I stalked through the forest, slaying the monsters as I found them. None of them put up any resistance. They were too dumb to know what was going on. They were just bloodsuckers—that was all they could do. I came upon their white soccer-ball-size eggs, singly or in clusters, stuck onto the side of hairs, and punctured every one I saw.

The longer it went on, though, the less I liked it. I'd thought this would be an adventure, but there was no excitement in it. And I kept having this unpleasant thought that in a way I was lowering myself to the level of the lice. They went around sucking blood and I went around stabbing them, and was there really much difference?

I'd killed about ten, I suppose, when I decided to call it a day. This could go on for a long time—Mom had announced she'd combed out eighty-five only the other night—and it was pointless. All I had to do was wish the lice were gone, after all. There was no need to personally hand-slaughter them.

So I wished Ben's head was clear of all lice and I wished that I was back to normal size and sitting on the toilet seat again.

"All gone?" Ben asked when I reappeared.

"All gone."

"Then where's my leopard helicopter?"

"Coming up."

So that was it. Everyone in my family had gotten what they wanted. Except me.

But what did I want?

Later that night, I was lying in bed, reading some Marvel comics I'd wished for. After a while, I got tired of reading and wished the superheroes and supervillains would come to life—but in miniature, the same size as they were in the comics—and act out their battles for me at the foot of my bed. It was fun watching the Fantastic Four slugging it out with Doctor Doom on my quilt.

I'd always wanted to be a superhero.

Yeah. *That* was what I wanted.

Chapter Eight

It was a pretty cool costume. I had a blue mask over my eyes, and a blue leotard, with blue boots, yellow tights, and a yellow cape. Oh yeah, and the blue leotard had yellow stars on it. I looked at myself in the mirror—I'd never had a full-length mirror in my room, but it was simple enough to wish for one—and thought, *Yeah, looks good.* The only things missing were the bulging muscles that superheroes tend to have, so I wished for a complete set: pecs, biceps, triceps, an awesome six-pack, the works. I looked at myself in the mirror again and was impressed. You wouldn't want to tangle with me.

Now I had to think of what superpowers to have. Ability to fly, obviously, that was a no-brainer. And superstrength, another gimme. What else, what else? The ability to go through walls like a ghost—that was a good one. And the power to run superfast, faster than a cheetah. And keep it up indefinitely. Better than a cheetah, because they get tired after a few hundred yards. I also wished for stretchy arms and legs like Mister Fantastic. And the ability to survive indefinitely without breathing, and to withstand extremes of heat and cold, and to be immune to pain, and have a body that automatically went diamond-hard if anyone hit me or kicked me or struck a blow of any kind. And I'd better be bulletproof and bombproof and fireproof, too, 'cause as a superhero I was bound to make a few enemies. That made me pretty much invincible. Finally, just for fun, I wished to be able to burrow underground like a mole.

Now I just had to think of a name.

Sam-Man?

Er, no.

Er . . .

Awesome Man?

Awesome Man!

Now to start crime-busting!

It was the morning after I'd gotten rid of Ben's lice and saved Dad's job, etc. Obviously, I'd need the day off from school to start my career as a superhero, so I wished the school was closed for the day because the boiler had broken down. I looked out of the window. It was a gray, drizzly day, which didn't look like it would be a whole lot of fun to fly through.

So I wished it was nice and sunny, sixty-eight degrees with a light breeze.

I tugged at the window to open it, but it was a little stiff. So I made a wish and it swung open obediently. I realized then that I'd never need to open a window manually again. Or a door. I could just wish they were already open. Actually, I didn't even need to do that. I didn't need windows or doors *at all*. I could just wish to be outside (or inside) whenever I wanted . . .

Anyway, I launched myself through the open window and flew out into the fresh morning air.

I stretched out my arms in front of me like Superman. I felt the wind rushing past my ears and my cape fluttering out behind me. The streets and trees and houses glided past below. I felt weightless and completely free. It was like those flying dreams I used to have when I was a little kid.

I scanned the streets below for crime. Not much going on down there, though. Shops opening up. People on their way to work, driving cars, hopping on and off buses. A few looked up and noticed me, and then more and more, and soon there were crowds of people gawping and pointing up at me. I waved at them.

Well, I flew around for a bit, waiting for something to kick off so I could fly down and stop it. Nothing happened. Well, nothing illegal. Listening to the news sometimes you'd think we lived in some sort of a war zone, with people being attacked and killed all over the place. It's not till you fly around above a whole town and watch it in action that you realize how law-abiding people are most of the time. They just go around getting on with their lives. No one even jumped a red light.

The morning dragged on. I got tired of waiting. I was sure there *must* be some crimes going on somewhere.

"I wish I was wherever the nearest person breaking the law is," I said aloud.

Whoosh! I landed on the sidewalk near a guy double-parking.

Hmm . . . It wasn't really the type of crime I'd been imagining. I mean, I don't think Batman gets called on the hotline whenever someone double-parks in Gotham City. I'd have preferred a bank job, to be honest. For a moment, I thought of wishing for one, but then I realized that would be pretty silly. A superhero who only solves crimes he's wished for himself. Like, Pointless Man.

Oh well. You have to work with what you get.

"Hold it," I said as the guy got out of his

car. He was wearing glasses and a suit and tie. "You can't park there."

"It's only for a minute; I need to get something in that shop—"

"Sorry, that's not allowed."

"Look, why don't you mind your own business?"

"It *is* my business, my friend; my duty is to uphold the law—"

"Are you a traffic cop?"

"You'll have to move that car."

"They've changed the uniform if you are!"

"Never mind about that—"

"That's the most ridiculous uniform I've ever seen. And we're paying for that out of our city taxes? It's a disgrace!"

"Look, I'm not a traffic cop—"

"Then what uniform is it?"

"It's not a uniform, it's a costume."

"A Halloween costume?"

"No, it's *my* costume. The costume of . . . *Awesome Man*!"

The guy started to look up and down the street. "This is one of those TV shows, isn't it. Where they play tricks on unsuspecting members of the public. Where are the cameras?"

"There aren't any cameras!"

"I bet they're in that van, aren't they." He started smiling and waving at a van on the other side of the street. "Hello, Mom!"

I was getting a little fed up. I didn't come into the superhero game for this sort of thing. Iron Man doesn't spend his time arguing with people on sidewalks, trying to get them to take him seriously, does he? It was . . . undignified. And it wasn't like I really cared where the guy parked his car anyway.

"All right," I said. "I've had enough of this. You can park your car where you like, but if you get a ticket, don't blame me."

And then I launched myself up from the sidewalk and zoomed into the sky. I glanced down when I was above roof height and the guy was goggling up at me in disbelief.

I flew on. I should explain about how it felt to fly. It didn't take any effort at all—it wasn't like swimming. I just pointed in the direction I wanted to fly and that's the direction I went in. And I could go faster or slower just by thinking about it. It was like if you decide to raise your hand, and it goes up—you don't really know how, it just does.

Then, at last, I looked down and saw something going on in an alley. Two figures, one big and one small, and the big one had pushed the little one up against a wall.

"This looks like a job for Awesome Man!" I said to myself.

I dived down and landed beside them with a thump.

The bigger one looked around with a start, and I recognized him.

"Hiya, Scorpus. Just thought I'd drop by."

He had one hand around the smaller boy's neck and the other hand clenched in a fist, cocked and ready to go. The smaller boy was a blond kid with pimples. Really bad pimples. Really inflamed. And I thought, *That's pretty bad luck—not only do you have a seriously bad skin day, but then you get mugged, too.*

Scorpus was like, "Who are you? How do you know my name?"

"I'm Awesome Man. Awesome Man knows all kinds of stuff!"

"Yeah? Well, get lost and mind your own business, and you won't get hurt!"

"*I* won't get hurt? It's you I'm worried about."

I grabbed hold of his arm and squeezed with my superstrength. Scorpus's pale face went even paler. He let go of the kid.

"Are you okay?" I said to the boy. "What was he doing to you?"

"Tryin' to steal my phone. And my money."

I turned to stare at Scorpus. I was still holding his arm, and I squeezed it a little tighter. Scorpus sucked in his breath and swore. He twisted and kneed me extremely hard in the groin. There was a painful-sounding *thunk*. Not painful to me, of course, because thanks to my superpowers my body had gone diamond-hard at the crucial moment.

Scorpus was like, "Aaaaghh!" He reeled off a string of swear words. "My knee. I think it's broke!"

"It's not broken at all, Scorpus! It's just

severely bruised. And serves you right any-way." I turned back to the kid. "Are you okay?" I asked again.

The kid nodded.

"Good. You can go, then. Oh, just one thing—I wish all your pimples were gone."

All the angry red pimples on his cheeks and chin vanished, leaving his skin all smooth and fresh, like a baby's butt. He put his hand up to his face and looked amazed. "Awesome!"

"All part of the service. That's why they call me . . . Awesome Man!"

The fresh-faced kid ran off down the alley.

"Now, what am I gonna do with you, Scorpus? You gotta stop mugging people. Mugging is . . . well, it's a mug's game!"

"Let . . . go . . . of . . . my arm." He spoke in little gasps, through gritted teeth.

I let go. His good arm rubbed the bad arm, while the bad arm massaged his knee.

"Why do you do it, Scorpus?"

He swore at me again. "Mind your own business, or I'll—"

"You'll never get anywhere being a mugger," I told him. "No one likes muggers. They never get rich. They never get awards or knighthoods. They don't get streets or buildings named after them. We don't put their pictures on money or anything."

"Who are you? I know that voice."

"It's me." I pushed my mask back onto my head. "Sam Polkinghorne. I already beat you up once, at school, remember?"

He narrowed his eyes and swore at me again.

"Swearing's the sign of a small vocabulary, Scorpus." (That's what my dad says, anyway. I don't know if it's true but I thought it sounded good.) "Now, let me ask you again. Why go around mugging people?"

"Let me put it like this," Scorpus began,

and then he suddenly jabbed me in the throat, with straight, stiff fingers. My diamond-hard powers kicked in automatically and he broke his fingernails. "Ow!" he howled. "Oooooowwwww!"

I started to lose patience. I gripped Scorpus around the middle and rose up into the air till we were level with the tops of the lampposts.

"Answer my question, Scorpus, or I'll drop you!"

"Help!" shouted Scorpus.

"You can help yourself, if you just answer me. Why do you do it?"

I felt Scorpus go limp. He stopped struggling and gave a great big sigh, as if he'd just given up on everything.

"I—I have to," he said.

"What do you mean? 'Course you don't have to."

"I do. I need the money."

"What for?"

"Everything! Food. Clothes. Sneakers. My phone."

"Your parents are supposed to buy those things . . ."

Scorpus laughed bitterly. "Yeah, right. My dad gives me nothing—*nothing*. Not even lunch money. He says I have to learn to fend for myself. Like he did."

"He wouldn't like it if he knew you were out robbing people."

"What're you talking about? '*Course* he'd like it."

Actually, from what I'd heard about Scorpus's dad, that was probably true. "But—what about your mom?"

Scorpus laughed that bitter laugh again. "If you think my mom would dare to disagree with my dad about anything—well, you don't know him, that's all."

"Well, what are we gonna do, then? You can't go on mugging people."

"I dunno. I got to eat, don't I?"

This was all getting a little more complicated than I'd expected. In the comics, superheroes just beat the villains up. They don't have to start solving their family problems. They simply don't get involved in that kind of thing.

"Will you put me down now?" said Scorpus.

I drifted to the ground again and let him go. "Listen," I said. "I'll give you some cash to tide you over." I wished for fifty pounds and gave it to him. "Suppose I go and see your dad—tell him to start being nice to you, feed you properly, give you an allowance. Would that be okay?"

Scorpus laughed. "Good luck with that!"

"Luck doesn't come into it," I said. "You're talking to Awesome Man!"

✷ ✷ ✷

Scorpus's home was a two-bedroom apartment in a run-down project on the edge of town. There was graffiti on the walls, garbage all over the ground, and scaly, diseased pigeons pecking in it. As I flew down, I wished it was all tidied up, with the garbage in garbage cans, the graffiti cleaned away, and the pigeons moved on. I also wished for some nice flower beds full of tulips, and for all the front doors to be newly painted in bright colors, so I'd done a pretty good job even before I knocked on Scorpus's door.

After I knocked there was a long pause. I hate waiting for things, always have, so I wished he'd come and open the door right away. (I'd never have to wait for anything again, I realized. No more hanging around at bus stops for buses that never came. Although, come to think of it, I'd never need to catch a bus again, either.)

The door was flung open and there stood Old Man—I realized I didn't know what his last name was and quickly wished that I did. *Bartrum*, the news anchor's voice in my head said. So, there stood Old Man Bartrum.

"Mr. Bartrum?"

He was a big man, tall and gangly with a sharp face like a hatchet. His head was shaved and his arms were covered in tats. His biceps were unexpectedly big and meaty, and I guessed he probably worked out. But he also had a bit of a paunch so I guessed he probably stopped at the fish and chips shop on the way home from the gym. He had a gold tooth in the front of his mouth.

"Who wants to know?"

"Me. Well, I don't wanna know 'cause I already know, actually. I've come to have a word with you."

"Who are you? And why are you dressed up like—what *are* you dressed up like? Some sort of cheerleader?"

"I'm Awesome Man and this is my costume—"

"Get lost." And he slammed the door on me.

I immediately wished it would bounce back open, of course.

He stood there glaring at me. "I said, get *lost*!"

Once again, he slammed the door and again I wished for it to bounce right back open.

"We can keep this up all day if you want," I said. "But why don't you just listen to what I have to say? It'll be quicker."

"I'll tell you what'll be quicker," Bartrum growled. You often read in books about people growling when they get angry. I'd never really heard it before. He deliberately deepened his voice and put a sort of gritty edge into it, if you know what I mean. "It'll be quicker if you just get out of here before you leave in an ambulance."

"I need to speak to you about your son—"

"You leave my boy out of this! He ain't done nothing, d'you hear me? And if he did, it ain't my fault. And I don't even have a son anyway. If you've come here to complain about him, I'll give you something to complain about! You come around here, knocking on my door—the nerve of it!"

I could see he was working himself into a fury. "Look," I said, "calm down—"

"Calm down? You're asking for a clock on the snot box!"

"No I'm not—"

And the next moment, he clocked me on the snot box. The nose, I mean. Which of course turned diamond-hard at the moment of impact.

Blood spurted from his knuckles. He staggered back, clutching his hand and cursing.

"I'll tell you what, Mr. Bartrum, why don't I come in and we can discuss this in a more civilized manner."

"We could do that, yeah, or we could try . . . *this*!"

He hit me as hard as he could in the stomach with his other hand and then doubled up in agony, each injured hand tucked beneath the opposite arm.

"Aaaargh!"

"Look, I'm sorry about this, but if you'd stop hitting me, you wouldn't keep hurting yourself. Tell you what. I wish we were sitting down in your living room."

The room was a mess. Empty beer cans and pizza boxes all over the place. I was sitting on an armchair that had a plate with crumbs on it, which I had to move out from under me. Old Man Bartrum was on the sofa opposite, staring at me with a combination of fear, hatred, and bewilderment.

"How did you do that?"

"I'm Awesome Man. It's all in a day's work for me. Listen, I want to talk to you about Scorpus. From what I hear, you treat him very badly. You don't give him any lunch money and he has to buy his own clothes."

"That's none of your business. And it's all lies."

"Is it, Mr. Bartrum? Is it?"

"Why don't you go away before I smash your face in?"

"Look, can't we just discuss this sensibly? What's the matter with you?"

"I've got anger management issues," Bartrum said. "That's what the prison psychologist told me."

"Oh yeah? And what did *you* say?"

"I didn't say nothing. I clocked him on the snot box."

I sighed. How was I ever going to get through to him? "Look, you've got to start being nicer to your son and your wife, okay?"

"I haven't got a wife."

"Well, your girlfriend or whatever. You gotta be nice to them."

"I'm always nice to them." He looked at me with big sincere eyes. "I'm a good person. Deep down."

"Is that right?"

"I tell you what," Bartrum said, suddenly completely changing his manner and smiling at me, his gold tooth glinting. "Do you want a cup of tea and a cookie? I got some Oreos."

I didn't really want tea and cookies, but it was the first sign of reasonable behavior he'd displayed, so I thought I'd better go along with it. "All right. Thanks."

He went out into the kitchen.

I called after him, "I just came to say, you've got to start treating your son better. Look after him, you know? Also, your girlfriend. I hear she's scared of you. That's not a healthy relationship, Mr. Bartrum."

All I could hear from the kitchen was the sound of rummaging around in cupboards.

"Are you listening to me, Mr. Bartrum?"

"Oh yes, I'm listening. It's very interesting, what you're saying."

Then he ran out of the kitchen with a frying pan in his hand and smashed me over the head with it.

The handle of the frying pan broke. Bartrum howled in pain and collapsed onto the sofa. The vibration of the impact must have hurt his already-damaged hand. And even I sort of grunted in discomfort. Of course, the frying pan hadn't actually hurt my diamond-hard head, but it made a very loud clanging noise, and the blow reverberated in my skull and made me feel dizzy.

What could you do with a person like this? He was an out-and-out psycho. There was no way I could persuade him to mend his ways, unless . . .

Of course. Unless.

"I wish you'd be nice to your son and partner, okay?"

"Okay," said Bartrum mildly.

"I wish you'd give them money when they need it, okay?"

"Okay."

There was silence. Mission accomplished, I realized.

"Well, I'll be off, then."

"Sure you won't stay for tea?"

"Nah, got a few things to do."

And I wished myself back in my bedroom.

Then I realized that my digestive system was actually feeling a bit cheated, so I wished for a nice cup of tea and a plate of Oreos.

Chapter Nine

As I drank the tea and ate the Oreos while sitting on my bed, I thought about being a superhero. There was something pointless about it when you had a million wishes at your disposal. Or almost a million, whatever it was. I'd solved the Bartrum problem just by wishing he'd be nice. I didn't need to go and confront the man. I could have done it sitting in my bedroom. I didn't need the costume, didn't need to be able to fly. Nor did I need the cheetah-like running speed or the stretchy arms and legs. I didn't need any of it.

I wished I didn't have the costume anymore. It was a silly costume anyway. And I wished away the superpowers, too. Because *they* were pointless as well. Flying had been fun for a while, but I didn't need it. Why fly anywhere? I could just wish I was already there. It was a shame, maybe, that I'd never gotten to use my burrowing powers. But again, what was the point of them? If I ever needed to get anything that was buried underground, I could just wish it was aboveground, not go squirming down after it like a giant mole.

My phone went off.

"Hi, Evan."

"Was that you who closed the school down today?"

"Yeah, I did that."

"Cool. What are you doing today?"

"Dunno. Wanna come over?"

"Yeah, sure."

"Hold on. I wish Evan was here."

He materialized in the middle of the bedroom, and his eyes immediately landed on the plate of Oreos. "Oh, good, can I have one?"

"Yeah, dig in."

There were three cookies left and he polished them off in about forty-five seconds. I wondered whether to wish for a few more for him but decided not to.

"Sam?"

"Yeah?"

"What I was saying yesterday—about guessing what I want you to wish for . . ."

To be honest, what with one thing after another, this had completely slipped my mind.

"I just wanted you to figure it out for yourself," Evan said. "I felt kind of awkward and—I sort of thought the wish might work better if it came from you. I dunno. But now—I have to ask you straight out . . ."

And then the whole scenario flashed into my mind. "Your dad!" I said.

Evan nodded. "My dad." His voice sort of quivered. "He's really sick, Sam." I looked and saw his eyes were full of silver tears. "He's dying."

"Oh, I . . . oh my God. Oh, Evan," I said.

I felt a horrible stab of guilt. Why hadn't I thought of this before? I knew how sick Evan's dad was. The last time I'd seen him was a few weeks ago, just after he came out of the hospital, and he looked really thin and gray and weak. The only thing I can say in my defense is that Evan didn't talk about it much, and when he mentioned his dad he tended to speak about things his dad said or did or liked, not about the illness. And in day-to-day life,

Evan seemed normal, having a laugh and a joke and playing games like everyone else. But maybe that's how people deal with it. The thought of Evan pretending to feel normal when all the time his heart was breaking inside made me feel even worse.

"Evan, I'm sorry," I said. "I should have realized. Of course I'll wish he's better!"

His face lit up like the sun breaking through rain clouds. If faces were skies, his would have had a rainbow all over it.

"Serious?"

"Yeah. Serious. I wish Evan's dad was completely better, right now!"

"And that's it?" Evan said.

"That's it!"

"He's better already?"

"That's what I wished for. And my wishes come true!"

"What's he doing?"

"Let's find out . . . I wish I knew what Evan's dad is up to."

The news anchor's voice intoned inside my head, *He's just thrown back the bedding, got up, and announced he's going to mow the lawn.*

I passed this on to Evan.

"That grass has gotten really high," Evan said. "I better go and give him a hand!"

"Do you want a few cookies to take?"

"Cookies? I don't need them *now*, do I?" And then I realized that it was only in the last couple of years, while his dad was ill, that Evan had gotten overweight. He must have been comfort-eating all that time.

"Wait a minute, though," Evan said. "I'll take some for my dad. I bet he'll have his appetite back!"

I wished for a speciality box of cookies with chocolate and icing, and pushed it into Evan's arms.

"Want me to wish you were there?" I asked.

"No, I . . . think I'll walk."

"Sure."

I watched him through the window as he left with the box of cookies under his arm. He didn't walk, though. He ran.

Chapter Ten

I'd done a good thing for Evan, even though I'd taken my time about it, and I felt kind of pleased with myself. I imagined him going home, seeing his dad, flying into his arms. I waited for a while, thinking Evan would text or phone about it, but he didn't, so I suppose he was too busy getting used to having his dad back in full health again, and I couldn't blame him.

I sat in my room and wondered what to do next. No one else was around. Ben and Maeve were at school, Dad was at work, and Mom was in the shed, getting her paintings ready for Bernard Souter. He was coming over tonight.

It was almost time for lunch, and I was feeling a little hungry. There's this dish Mom sometimes makes, Chicken Supreme, which is pieces of chicken breast in a white, creamy sauce with rice, and I really like it. I don't know what made me think of it just then, but I wished for a big plate of it. I was about to eat it on a tray on my knees, sitting on my bed, and then I thought, *Come on, you can do better than that*, so I wished I was watching a soccer game in the director's box at White Hart Lane, watching Tottenham Hotspur play Arsenal. I had the box all to myself, and I wished Spurs would win seven-nothing, and I scarfed down the Chicken Supreme, listening to the roar of the crowd as the goals flew in.

Which was kind of fun. But not as much fun as it would have been if I hadn't wished for it. Of course, if I hadn't wished for it, it wouldn't have happened. The trouble was, it wasn't a surprise. Once I'd made the wish, it was, you know, inevitable, just like Wednesday following Tuesday.

And I realized that surprises were a thing of the past for me, now that I had my wishes. No surprises, no suspense, no uncertainty. No feeling of joy at an unexpected piece of good luck. No sense of relief when something that looked like it was going to turn out badly turned out okay. Reality wasn't something I could bump into anymore. It was something that did what I told it.

Was that even a good life?

The referee blew his whistle when the game was over. I wished that Tottenham would win the Premier League that season. At least that would surprise quite a few people, even if I wasn't one of them.

I wished myself back in my bedroom. I was actually starting to feel a little bored, which is ridiculous when you've got almost a million wishes at your disposal. What could I do?

The superhero thing. Maybe I hadn't explored that thoroughly yet. Obviously, Scorpus and Old Man Bartrum weren't worthy opponents. They were pushovers. I needed someone who was more of a match for me.

Most superheroes have some kind of archenemy. Like, Batman has the Joker and Spider-Man has the Green Goblin and the Fantastic Four have Doctor Doom. And the archenemies have the power to hurt them, threaten them, frustrate them. The superhero always wins in the end, but the archenemy can give them a pretty hard time along the way. And even when the superhero finally triumphs, the archenemy usually slips away with a promise to come back and make trouble another day. That's part of the fun of it.

I needed an enemy who could fight back.

First, I wished for all my powers back, the same ones as before, but I gave myself a different costume. I wished I was dressed all in black leather, with lots of silver studs and stars and stuff, and a big silver letter *A* on my chest. I thought it looked a little tougher. More manly.

Now I needed an archenemy.

This was going to be fun. You know, I've often thought when I finish school I'd like to get a job writing stories for comics. Come to think of it, I could just wish that was my job, if I was serious. But I dunno. I didn't *need* a job, did I?

I forced my thoughts back to my archenemy. I wished first of all that he could fly and was superstrong. But he needed something different, something to make him unique . . . I thought back to Bartrum hitting me with a frying pan. How about if my archenemy had frying pans for hands? No, something a bit deadlier, maybe. Hammers! With which he battered his opponents. Superstrong hammers that didn't break. Hammer Man? Hammerhand? No, wait, *one* hand could be a hammer. The other one could be a circular saw. And suddenly I got the whole concept: Power-Tool Man! His head was a pneumatic drill. His body was a workbench. His legs were those things that workmen use to flatten asphalt. What are they called? Pile drivers— that's it.

"I wish Power-Tool Man existed, and I wish he was coming to get me!"

There was a splintering crash as my bedroom door flew off its hinges.

There stood Power-Tool Man. His power-drill head was pointing straight at me, twirling around and around. His circular-saw arm was raised.

"Hello, Mr. so-called Awesome Man!" he said in a horrible, whiny drill voice. "Let us see how awesome you are ven you are all smeshed into liddle tiny bits." He had a German accent; I don't know why.

"Bring it on, Power-Tool Man. If you think you're hard enough."

"Oh, *ja*, I sink I vill be hard enoff to deal vid you. My power-tools are all diamond-tipped, you know."

Diamond-tipped! The only thing hard enough to cut another diamond!

He lunged at me with unexpected speed. I dodged, and his whirring drill bit missed me by inches. As he went past I clouted him with all my force on the side of his head. He fell onto my bed, and his circular saw ripped the mattress in two. Before he could regain his footing, I leaped on him, grabbed him by the arms, and flew out of the window with him.

As we zoomed up into the clear blue sky, he smashed me repeatedly on the side of the head with his hammer-hand. The diamond-tipped hammer was making dents in me, I could feel it. That couldn't be good.

"You like dis, *ja*?"

"Not much—but tell me how you like . . . *this*!"

We were about a hundred yards up in the air, and I let go of him. I expected him to fall and hit the ground with a sickening clang, but somehow I'd forgotten that he could fly, just like me, so instead of falling he just looped-the-loop, came up behind me, and gave me a massive kick with one of his pile-driver legs. I flew across the sky, out of control, arms waving helplessly.

"*Ja*, I am liking dis. It is *sehr gut!*"

"I wish you'd stop talking in that stupid accent!"

"What stupid accent?" he said in a perfectly normal English accent.

"I'm not here to give you elocution lessons, Power-Tool Man. I'm here to knock you into a pile of scrap metal!"

I steadied myself, thrust my fists out in front of me, and power-dived at him at top speed. He didn't try to get out of the way but flew straight toward me.

We met with a tremendous clatter in the middle of the sky and bounced apart. But he recovered first. I was still spinning in the air when I felt his drill bite into my chest. At the same time the circular saw started to chew into my neck, and the hammer-hand was whacking me on the back of the head.

This was . . . too much. "I wish you couldn't fly anymore, Power-Tool Man," I shouted, and immediately he plunged away from me and spiraled toward the earth. He hit the ground with a crash that was loud even from a hundred yards up.

He wasn't hurt, though, what with being superstrong. He bounced straight back up onto his feet. I zoomed down toward him. He started winding his hammer-hand up, whirling it around to get ready for a mighty blow. But I wasn't having it. "I wish you were as weak as a kitten!" I said. So he stood there, all helpless and tottering, not strong enough even to raise his power-tool arms. I landed beside him and gave him a little push in his workbench-chest and he fell on his back.

"Do you surrender, Power-Tool Man?"

"No, I'll never surrender!"

"I wish you would."

"Oh, all right, I surrender."

"Another awesome victory for Awesome Man!" I said. But it didn't feel all that awesome. I was fed up. "I wish you didn't exist anymore, Power-Tool Man."

"I don't."

And he was gone.

* * *

I wished my bedroom was all back to normal again. Then I went downstairs to watch TV for a little while, and amused myself by making the actors and talk show hosts say stupid things and insult each other. So that was pretty funny. It passed the time, anyway.

Things looked up a little later when my family started coming home. Mom went to get Ben from school at three. He was in a supergood mood, excited about his day.

"Guess what happened at school, Sam?" he shouted as soon as he got into the hall. Obviously, I knew what had happened 'cause I'd wished for it, but I said, "What?"

"I got put in the top group for Literacy!"

"You did?"

"He did," Mom said. "Miss Martinez said she'd never seen anything like it. She said he was reading aloud from *Great Expectations*!"

"Where'd you get that from?"

"Dunno, I just found it in my backpack. I dunno where it came from. But I can read it! I can read anything! I just look at the words and they all make sense. It's like magic!"

"Cool."

"They did a test," my mom said. "Miss Martinez says he's got a reading age of fourteen!"

"Yeah, and Fatima was really fed up!" Ben added. He started dancing around the hall, chanting, "In your face, Fatima!" until Mom gave him a little prod to make him shut up.

Ben went upstairs to play with his new remote-controlled helicopter. What he didn't know was I'd wished for a miniature leopard to pilot it, and the leopard could talk and say things like, "Altitude two thousand feet" and "Just bringing her in for a landing," and wave its paw at him as it flew by. I listened outside his room and heard his squeaks of excitement.

"Sam!" he said. "Come and see this!"

I went in and saw the little leopard flying around. "Excellent weather conditions for flying today!" it squeaked. "Hello, Ben!"

"This is the best helicopter ever!" Ben said.

"Yeah, but don't tell Mom and Dad about it. It's our secret."

"Why? 'Cause it's magic?"

"Yes, Ben. 'Cause it's magic."

* * *

When Maeve got home from school she was in a supergood mood, too.

She ruffled my hair as she came into the living room. "Everything all right, Sam?"

"Yeah, fine."

"How was school?"

"We got the day off today. Boiler broke down."

"That was a lucky break, wasn't it? Still, it's not too bad there, is it?"

"It's okay."

"Listen, I'm sorry if I talked it up a bit, you know. I was only teasing."

"No worries. How was your day?"

"Fantastic!"

"Why?"

I knew why, obviously, because I'd made a few wishes, but I wanted to hear how they'd worked out.

It was all going swimmingly with Stefan Bumgarner. He was totally crazy about her and went around holding her hand all day, which he never used to like doing, but now it was as if he wanted to advertise his love to the whole world. Also, he'd bought them both tickets to see some weird French circus where they ride motorbikes on tightropes and juggle chainsaws to the accompaniment of loud rock music and crazy laser displays, which she'd always wanted to see.

"Sounds great."

"Yep. Life's sweet!" She smiled, and I

realized how pretty she was when her face wasn't all creased up in a scowl.

Mom was in the kitchen, cooking supper and singing at the top of her lungs. She couldn't wait for Bernard Souter to turn up.

A key turned in the front door and my dad came in. I went into the hall to greet him.

"Hey, Sam!" He gave me a hug. "You'll never believe what happened to me today!"

"What?"

"I have to tell your mom this!" I followed him into the kitchen. "Roger Haggerston came to my office today, and he said I was so good at my job that he wanted to promote me—to *his* job! He's going to step down, because he says he knows I'm the better man!"

"Did he really say that?"

"His exact words. 'You're the better man by far,' he said."

"Amazing!"

"My salary's going to double, and I'm going to have a much bigger office, with a beverage cabinet and a view of the river."

"Fantastic!"

The doorbell rang. Mom ran to open it, and it was Bernard Souter. He was wearing white trousers and a cream-colored jacket and a sort of candy-striped shirt.

"Good evening, Mr. Souter!"

"Oh, please, you must call me Bernard. And I shall call you Susan!"

"Well, you could, but my name's actually Nicola."

"I beg your pardon, Nicola. Yes, Nicola Polkinghorne is a name that the world will soon know very well indeed! Your wonderful work is like a breath of fresh air in a stale and dusty mausoleum!"

"Yes, that's the effect I've been striving for," said Mom.

"And where are the pictures? Let us delay no further, I am athirst, I am agog!" He had just about the fanciest voice I'd ever heard.

Mom led him through the kitchen and down the yard to the shed at the end. We all trooped after them to hear what he was going to say. Well, in my case, I knew, but I still trooped along to actually hear him say it.

He walked along the line of paintings, giving little groans and gasps of pleasure and appreciation. He stopped in front of a still life of a loaf of bread on a breadboard with a dish of butter next to it and some crumbs. "Remarkable!" he murmured. He moved on to a picture of a blackbird on a lawn, casting a long shadow that made it look like it was on stilts. "Wonderful!" Next, he feasted his eyes on a portrait of Ben, which did look like him, but also like a kind of evil goblin. "Stupendous!"

I should say here that I really don't know much about art, and to be honest, I don't know how good my mom's stuff is. But the paintings were all done in nice bright colors and looked more or less like what they were supposed to look like. They looked okay to me. I don't know about "stupendous," but I've seen worse stuff in galleries, you know?

"Contemporary British art is moribund," Bernard announced. "Twitching in its death throes! These wonderful paintings will sweep all that arid, self-indulgent, conceptual nonsense aside. It will be a new dawn for British art—a revolution!"

"Oh, well, you know, that's very nice of you," Mom said, all grinning and blushing.

"So you think there's enough here for an exhibition?" my dad said.

"Oh, certainly, certainly. *Certainement!* I have arranged for a major exhibition at the Tate Modern—and I can assure you it will make everything else there look suddenly very old-fashioned indeed! Now, I am sure that all these pictures will sell, and will fetch very high prices indeed. I am not a rich man—but could I perhaps be permitted the liberty of putting in a bid for one of these wonderful paintings before the exhibition? Otherwise, I fear I shall be swept aside in the rush!"

"Take your pick!" said my mom.

"An impossible decision . . . For the first time in my life I truly understand the full force of the expression 'spoiled for choice' . . . But on the whole, all things considered, I think . . . this one!" He pointed to the one of the bird with the long-legged shadow. "How much, dear lady?"

Mom and Dad looked at each other. "What do you think?" said my dad.

"Er, fifty pounds?" suggested my mom.

"Nonsense!" said Bernard. "A trifling, piffling sum!"

"Well, I don't know then," my mom said. "What about a hundred?"

"Surely you jest? The painting is worth many times that!"

"Five hundred?" my dad said.

"Nowhere near enough!"

"All right, then," said my mom. "A thousand!"

"You are determined to rob yourself!"

"Five thousand?"

"Make it ten thousand, and we have a deal!" He took out his checkbook and a silver fountain pen and made out a check to Nicola Polkinghorne on the spot. Then he placed a little sticky red dot on the frame of the picture. "That is to signify the painting has been sold, and after the exhibition it will come to me!"

"That's fantastic, Mom!" Maeve said.

"He should have picked the one of me," Ben said.

"You're right!" Souter said suddenly. "That is indeed a wonderful painting and I would be an abject fool not to purchase it while I have the opportunity!" Out came the checkbook and fountain pen again. "Shall we say ten thousand for this one, too?"

Chapter Eleven

I lay in bed the next morning trying to decide whether to go to school or not. Obviously, I could have had the day off, or as many days as I wanted. In fact, I never needed to go to school again if I didn't feel like it. But I decided in the end to go, just for something to do. I didn't bother with all that getting-up stuff, though, that was a waste of time. I just wished I was already up and dressed and washed and all that. I never needed to do any of that stuff again. That was one of the weird things about having all these wishes—I kept discovering new things I'd never need to do again.

And the thought crossed my mind: Was there *anything* I needed to do now?

As I went downstairs, I could hear Mom singing, " 'Oh, what a beautiful morning, oh, what a beautiful day!' " When I went into the kitchen she was all smiles, and so were Ben and Maeve. (Dad had already left—he couldn't wait to get to his enormous new office with the river view.) It really did make an amazing difference to get up in the morning and see everyone in a good mood, because to be honest, at that time of day everyone in our house normally looks about as happy as a bloodhound with a stomachache.

"What do you want for breakfast, Sam?"

"I wish for a full English breakfast."

"Oh, don't be silly, there's no time for that—"

" 'Course there is. Look, it's already done!" I pointed at the heaped plate—bacon, eggs, sausages, black pudding, beans, mushrooms, grilled tomatoes, fried bread—that had appeared on the breakfast table.

"What? How did that get there?"

"I wish no one cared about that."

They all lost interest immediately. I scarfed down the breakfast, and afterward I felt really sluggish, but then I wished I felt fine, not full but not hungry, either, so that was all right.

The doorbell rang, and it was Evan. There was a glow of happiness on his face. It's amazing the difference being happy makes to someone's face. You can't put your finger on it and say what feature's actually changed, but they just look *better* all around. Sharper. Brighter.

"How'd it go?" I said. "With your dad?"

"Oh, Sam, it's just . . . incredible. It's—I can't put it into words, it's like I had a . . .

terrible injury, and now it's healed. I'm just . . . *so glad* he's like he used to be again! The doctors have no idea how it happened! Thanks so much!"

"Oh, that's okay. No worries."

Evan's face went thoughtful. "There's not . . . any sort of a catch, is there?"

"What d'you mean?"

"I mean, like, in stories when people wish, there's usually a catch. You know, it backfires, or you have to pay for it in some way."

"Not with my wishes! I wish for it, I get it, that's it! End of story."

We walked on in silence for a while.

"What else are you gonna wish for?" Evan asked. "Don't you want anything for yourself?"

"I guess."

"What, then?"

"I don't know."

* * *

That was the problem. I really *didn't* know.

It seemed to me that other people had gotten a lot more happiness out of my wishes than I had, so far. And I didn't begrudge them that—in fact, I got pleasure out of their happiness. But things I wanted for myself—well, it was just so easy to get them that it didn't seem to mean very much.

At school that day, for instance, I got top marks in Math. Well, big deal.

I went along to the chess club at lunchtime and beat everyone there in simultaneous games, including Steve Rubenstein, who's played for the county. Again, big deal.

In PE we played soccer and I scored fifteen goals. Great.

In the afternoon, I got bored in Science— I'd wished I understood everything about the parallax effect, so the teacher, Mr. Qadir, was telling me stuff I already knew—so I just wished the bell would ring an hour early.

Probably the best thing that happened at school was that Scorpus came up and said, "Whatever you done to my old man, man, thanks! He's a different person now." So that was good. But again, that was another thing I'd done for someone else. What about *me*?

After school I watched TV with Ben and made everyone say ridiculous things again. So on Animal Planet, when one of the presenters was trying to talk about a safari park where they were trying to get white rhinos to breed, I had the other presenter keep coming in front of her and singing, "Old MacDonald Had a Farm." And then on *Nick News* I wished they'd report everything in sausage-and-mash—you know, that game where every time you get a word beginning with *s* you say *sausage* and every time it begins with *m* you say *mash*. So this report about the European Space Agency became a report about the European Sausage Agency. And they said that the European Sausage Agency was hoping to put a sausage rocket on the mash, and they'd be able to find out a great deal about the mash of sausage. Then there was a quiz show and I wished one of the teams would answer *custard* to every question while the other team answered *butt*. It was pretty funny. Ben was in fits.

But.

The problem was that all this stuff was, like, trivial, you know? It was kind of fun—well, yeah, it *was* fun, let's be fair, but it was still sort of . . . unsatisfying.

I thought about it later that evening as I was floating around my bedroom (I'd wished for it to be zero gravity in my room, just for a change) and drinking a root beer I'd wished for. At first everything—all the furniture and the root beer—went floating around the room as well, until I wished for it all to behave normally but for the room to be zero grav just as far as *I* was concerned, so that was all right.

I still didn't know what I really wanted. The problem was, it almost didn't make sense to want things anymore. Because how can you want something when you can just get it, immediately, just by asking for it? When there's no gap between wanting something and getting it, then getting it doesn't mean anything. There's no tension. No relief or surprise or sudden joy.

The most successful wishes, I realized, were the ones where I did good stuff for other people. Because when you unexpectedly get good stuff from someone else's wish, then it *does* mean something—there's room to feel surprise, relief, or sudden joy. So maybe I should think of some more wishes to help other people?

And try thinking bigger. I mean, I could make Scorpus's dad a nicer person just by wishing for it. I could cure people with terminal illnesses! I shouldn't be wasting my wishes on making people on children's TV say silly things to make Ben laugh. With all the power I had, I should be doing something much more serious.

But . . . what?

And then I had an idea so big it took my breath away.

How about this: What if I wished that *everyone on earth was nice all the time?*

People being polite and kind and generous to each other all the time. All over the world. Think about it. No more wars, no more violence, not even anyone being snippy or snarky or snitty or sarcastic anymore.

That was certainly a pretty big idea. But as soon as I'd had it, I had *another* idea, and it was even more colossal, and took my breath away even more than the first one.

What if I wished that *no one would die ever again?*

Let's face it, the fact that everybody does have to croak sooner or later is a major downer. But without death—no more funerals, no more orphans, no more grieving and mourning . . .

Plus everyone being nice . . .

That would be heaven on earth, wouldn't it?

I didn't stop to think. "I wish everyone on earth was as nice as possible to everyone else all the time. And I wish people would stop dying."

After that I felt a bit tired. It had been a busy day. So I wished my teeth were brushed and I was lying in bed in silk pajamas. I couldn't wait for the next day to see how my wishes had changed the world.

I closed my eyes, wished myself pleasant dreams, and wished to fall asleep in ten seconds.

Chapter Twelve

"Good morning, Sam. You look good today!" Maeve said.

"Do I?"

"Yeah, really handsome."

"Thanks; you look really pretty."

"You both look lovely!" Mom said.

"You all look absolutely wonderful!" said my dad.

"So do you, Dad," said Ben. "And you don't just *look* wonderful, you *are* wonderful!"

I chimed in. "You're wonderful, too, Ben!"

"We're all wonderful!" said my mom.

"Everyone in the world is wonderful!" Maeve said—and at that precise moment, and I hadn't even wished for this, the radio started playing that old Louis Armstrong song, "What a Wonderful World," and we all burst out laughing.

The doorbell rang and it was Evan. "Hi, Sam. It's so good to see you! You're my best friend and I really, really like you!"

"I really, really like you, too, Evan!"

"Actually, I really like everyone!"

"So do I, 'cause everyone's really nice!"

"They are, you're right, that's totally correct."

"So really, *everyone's* our best friend!"

"You're right, Sam! That's an incredibly perceptive comment."

"Thanks. And you're incredibly perceptive, too, Evan."

On the way to school, total strangers kept smiling at us and calling out, "Good morning!" We passed two drivers who were arguing, in the nicest possible way, about who should have a parking space—each one was trying to insist that the other should have it.

At school, everyone was opening doors for each other and trying to get the other person to go through first. It created quite a few traffic jams in the halls. Even Scorpus was being nice. I saw him carrying Tiffany Johnson's books for her, while jabbering on about how lovely and glossy her hair was. In Geography, Miss Skelmersdale gave us a test, but also gave out all the answers at the same time because, she said, she didn't want anyone to feel bad about not getting top marks.

At lunchtime, I played soccer. I'd already made a wish to be amazing at soccer yesterday, but today I wished everyone else was just as amazing as me, otherwise they might get upset, and I couldn't bear that. It was sort of a peculiar game. Early on, I was running down the wing with the ball at my feet and Iqbal Patel moved in to tackle me. I thought I could maybe flick the ball past and run around him—but then, if I succeeded, he'd feel humiliated. No, it would be better if I let him tackle me, 'cause then he'd feel good about himself. I pushed the ball a little too far forward so he had the chance to snatch it off my toes—but he slowed down and kind of waved for me to go past him. I stopped and made a sort of be-my-guest gesture, pointing at the ball.

"No, you go, bro."

"No, it's okay, you can tackle me."

"No, man, you keep the ball, you deserve it."

"But so do you!"

We kind of smiled at each other. Iqbal said, "Why don't we give it to someone else?"

"Yeah, you're right, it's good to share. Shall we give it to Evan?"

"Yeah, I like Evan, he's a good guy."

"One of the best."

I passed it to Evan (who was on Iqbal's team) and he ran toward the goal with it. As he got to the edge of the penalty area, all the defenders melted away to give him a clear shot. And our goalie walked away from the goal and leaned on the post with his arms folded.

He nodded pleasantly at Evan. "There you go. It's all yours."

All the defenders applauded this generous gesture.

"Go on, Evan!" I shouted. "Score!"

"No, I can't," said Evan. "Then it would be one to zero and you guys would be really upset."

"No, honestly, we don't mind!" I said.

"Don't score, Evan," Iqbal advised him. "It wouldn't be fair to them."

"You're right." Evan carefully kicked the ball wide of the goal. Now it was his own team's turn to applaud.

The game ended in a zero to zero tie. It wasn't very exciting. But it was very good-natured.

When I got home from school, Mom was on the phone. "No, I quite understand," she was saying. "I totally agree with you. I think this shows how sensitive and empathetic you are, and I admire you for it."

"Hello, lovely Mother. Who was that?" I asked as she hung up.

"Hello, darling Sam. That was the marvelous Bernard Souter. He was just saying he feels really guilty about all the artists he's ever given bad reviews to, and he wants to make amends. So he'd like to ask them all if they want to share my exhibition. I said yes, of course."

"How many of them are there?"

"About five thousand."

"Gonna be a little crowded."

"Yes—but think how hurt anyone would be if they were left out!"

"You're right, Mom," I said. "You're dead right."

✱ ✱ ✱

I was in the kitchen, eating a seafood salad that I'd wished for, when Maeve came in.

"Hello, darling little brother."

"Hi, beautiful sister. Did you have a lovely day?"

Maeve started crying, but she was also sort of smiling through the tears. "Yes, it was lovely, thanks, but . . . difficult. I had to tell Stefan he could go out with Josephine Waxwing again. She was so upset when he dumped her and I just knew it wasn't fair. She's such a nice person."

"Oh, poor Maeve! So he's dumped *you* instead?"

"No, we came to an arrangement. She's going to go out with him on Mondays, Wednesdays, and Fridays, and I have him on Tuesdays, Thursdays, and Saturdays."

"What about Sundays?"

"That's his day off. But I go out with Stanley Jollop then. He's liked me for years and I can't bear to disappoint him. He's so nice."

"Oh, good, so that's all straightened out. That was really smart of you."

Maeve shook her head. "I don't know, though—am I doing enough to make everyone happy? There may be other boys who want to go out with me, too, and I can't bear the thought of disappointing them!"

"There's bound to be other boys who want to go out with you!" I said. "Hundreds of them. Because you're so nice!"

"D'you think I should go out with all of them?"

"Well, it'll be difficult, but I suppose you should . . ."

Maeve thought about this. "I'll have to organize some sort of rotation . . ."

A little later, when Dad came home from work, he told us he'd invited Roger Haggerston and everyone else who worked in the building to share his office with the river view with him.

We all agreed he'd done the right thing. But it did occur to me that I'd created a pretty weird world.

And I wasn't quite sure how it was going to work out.

Chapter Thirteen

Normally, I don't watch the news. It's either really boring, about things I don't understand, like politics and interest rates, or it's full of horrible, scary stories about people getting bashed, beaten, brutalized, butchered, or blown up.

Frankly, I don't know why they put it on. They're either crazy or they think everyone else is crazy. No one but a psychopath could enjoy it. And it's not just once a week, like most programs, but every single day. Several times a day, in fact. The whole thing's insane.

But what I'm leading up to is that on this particular day I did settle down on the sofa at six o'clock with a Coke and a slice of pizza and, just for a change, turned on the news. I knew no crimes would have been committed now that everyone was nice, so I was curious to see what they'd fill the program with.

The news anchor, a guy with a pink tie with purple swirls on it, was all happy and smiley. "Today's extraordinary story, which is being confirmed from all around the world, is that, for the first time in human history, a day has passed on which nobody seems to have died, anywhere on the globe. Not one death has been recorded in the last twenty-four hours in any hospital in the United Kingdom. The story is the same throughout the European Union, and other countries are confirming the same remarkable phenomenon. Angela Crudgington reports."

Cut to a woman with a mic, standing outside a big hospital with a fleet of ambulances in the background. The wind whipped her blond hair around her face. Another guy in a white coat with a stethoscope around his neck was standing beside her. "I'm at Whipps Cross, the largest hospital in East London, with a patient population of some three thousand people and many times that number of outpatients, as well as a busy Accident and Emergency department, which sees hundreds of patients a day. In a normal twenty-four-hour period, doctors say the hospital would expect to lose a number of patients. But no one has died since yesterday. A freak statistic—or evidence of something far more mysterious?

"I have with me the very charming, intelligent, and handsome Dr. Wickramasinghe—he really is a great guy, there's no question about that." She pushed the mic under the doctor's nose. "Dr. Wickramasinghe—how do you account for this?"

Dr. Wickramasinghe said, "Thanks, Angela. I'd just like to say first of all that you are an extremely good-looking and talented interviewer! Well, we can't account for it at this stage. If this hospital alone was involved, I'd say we'd just had a good day—it's not unheard of to have a twenty-four-hour period in which no one dies. But two things make this very strange indeed. First, several colleagues have told me of individual cases involving terminally ill patients who really seemed unlikely to make it through this last day, but every single one of them has hung on. But second, and this is the truly amazing thing, it appears that no hospital in the country or—and this seems frankly incredible—*in the world* has reported any deaths for this period. That's got to be more than just a freak statistic."

"So what's your explanation?"

"That's a great question, Angela. But I don't have an explanation."

"Could it be that, well, people have just *stopped dying*? We might all live forever?"

"Well, that's impossible, of course."

"So what's the explanation?"

"I told you, I don't have one."

The interviewer looked a little confused. "This is Angela Crudgington in East London. Back to you in the studio, Martin."

"Thank you, Angela. I have with me the very intelligent and extremely nice population expert Dr. Timothy Wendover, from the University of East Anglia."

The guy with him looked like a typical eccentric professor, with a wild, unruly beard and a small pair of glasses that sat crookedly on his nose. "Good evening," he said. "I really like your tie, by the way. That's a very attractive pattern. Good choice."

"Thanks very much. It's really kind of you. So, Dr. Wendover, this is something quite unprecedented, isn't it?"

"It is totally unprecedented. Usually, thousands of people die worldwide every *hour*. The idea that even for an hour nobody would die is frankly bizarre—and a whole day seems outright impossible. And yet that is apparently the case. Assuming these early reports are reliable. And they do seem to be."

"So it has come as a total surprise—there were no indications of a decrease in death rates prior to this?"

The professor swept the suggestion away with both hands and his glasses slipped down his nose a bit farther. "Not *at all*. In fact, there has actually been an upward trend in deaths per day, as the world population continues to grow. This has come out of nowhere and we have no way of accounting for it."

"Could it be connected with improved medical care—better medicines and hygiene standards . . . ?"

"That's a very smart suggestion," said Dr. Wendover. "It was clever of you to make it and I hope you won't be offended when I say that can't be the explanation. In the first place, the change is far too sudden and extreme to be explained in that way. And in the second place, rates of illness and accident haven't changed. It's not as if everyone has suddenly gotten better. People who were terminally ill yesterday are still terminally ill. People all over the world were admitted to the hospital after car crashes and other accidents, many with terrible injuries that would normally be fatal—but somehow *nobody died.*"

That made me feel a bit queasy. I hadn't thought of that. All those people lying in intensive care who, by rights, should have been dead, hanging on to life when they maybe didn't even want to. That hadn't occurred to me when I made the wish.

"Some have suggested that something miraculous has occurred," the news anchor was saying. "That a profound change has taken place and humans are no longer mortal. It sounds far-fetched, I know, but could there be any possibility . . . ?"

"Good question. You're right to pose it. An event as bizarre as this naturally encourages us to seek bizarre explanations. But it is of course impossible that we could have become immortal, unless the laws of biology have all been canceled."

"But suppose that had happened—would that be good news for the human race?"

Dr. Wendover looked serious and sorrowful. "You might think so, and believe me I understand why you might think that. But if true, that would be an utter disaster."

I leaned forward a little. What did he mean, an *utter disaster*?

"You see, while death rates have stopped—at least temporarily—birth rates have not," Dr. Wendover went on. "So the world's population would rise very, very fast indeed. Soon there would be food shortages. Water shortages. Shortages of all resources. But still no one would die. People who were starving would simply keep on starving. But not dying. And because illness has not stopped, either, you'd have lots of people suffering from disease, but the disease would never kill them. They'd just keep on suffering for eternity. It would, in fact, be hell on earth."

He was so upset by this prospect that he burst into tears.

So did the news anchor.

And so did I.

I'd screwed up with that last wish. Big time. I hadn't meant to cause all these problems.

Problems.

Problems.

Problems *were* the problem, weren't they?

A lightbulb went on above my head.

What if there were no more problems?

Through my sobs, I said, "I wish there were no more problems in the world!"

And then everything went quiet.

Chapter Fourteen

You're not normally aware of it, but there's always some kind of noise going on in the background, even when it's quiet. If there are other people in the house, you hear them moving around or breathing; you hear the radio in a muffled kind of way from distant rooms; you hear the hum of the fridge; you hear sounds from the street outside, dogs barking, people walking past, and cars vrooming along, etc., etc.

But now all that had stopped. Cut off, abruptly, as if someone had hit the mute button.

"Mom? Dad?"

Silence.

I went out into the hall. "Maeve? Ben?"

No answer.

"Billiam?"

They'd all been in the house a minute ago. Maeve was up in her room, presumably on Facebook, Dad was taking a bath, Ben was helping Mom cook in the kitchen (he likes doing that), and Billiam was hanging around their feet, hoping they'd drop something he could eat ("If it goes to the ground, it belongs to the hound," that's what we say in our house). But now they'd all disappeared. Where?

It was kind of freaky. I went outside onto the street. Everything was there, as usual, all the houses with cars parked outside and garbage cans in the front yards. Clouds were slowly drifting across the sky, so it wasn't like everything had stopped moving. But there didn't seem to be any people. No birds sang. What was going on?

I walked into the center of town. I didn't see a living thing. No dogs or cats. Not even any insects. I got to the High Street and all the shops were there as usual but nobody was in them. I stepped into the big supermarket, Sainsbury's, and the automatic doors swished open to let me in, and there were all these aisles of fruit and vegetables and stuff, and Muzak playing softly, but there were no customers and nobody at the registers. Not a soul in sight. It was kind of eerie.

I didn't like being on my own anymore. "I wish Evan was here."

Evan appeared in front of me. I felt incredibly relieved to see him. But he looked seriously confused. "Sam! What's going on? Where is everybody?"

"I was hoping you might be able to tell me. Where have you just come from?"

"I don't know! I was watching TV, that amazing news story about how everyone's stopped dying—and I was just thinking, I bet Sam's got something to do with this, and then everything went black. And now I'm here. Come on, what did you wish?"

"I wished there were no problems in the world."

Evan's confused expression morphed into the lost-in-thought one. His hands went to his mouth. "That's quite a wish, Sam!"

"I suppose it is," I agreed. "But how could it make everyone disappear?"

"Well, the thing is, there are always problems in life, aren't there?" Evan said. "I mean, there's got to be. Figuring out what's the best thing to do. Making choices. Dealing with stuff. But if there are no people—then there are no problems!"

"So it's like this all over the world?"

"Must be. That was the only way of making sure there could never be any problems!"

There was a pause as we both thought about this huge planet, completely deserted except for us two. Skyscrapers, street markets, sports stadiums, shopping malls, city squares, all as quiet and empty as the Sahara Desert.

"But what about all the animals?" I said. "They don't have problems."

"Of course they do! Say you're a cat, and you're getting bullied by the tomcat next door. Or you're a fox and you can't find any food. Or you're a slug and a hedgehog is trying to eat you . . ."

"Hmm. I guess . . ."

"The only way you could have a world without problems is if you had a world without life, right? Like, there are no problems on Mars, are there? 'Cause there's nobody there to have them!"

Looked like I'd messed up again.

"I know you're trying to help," Evan said. "That's 'cause you're such a nice guy. You want to make the world a better place. That's good."

"That's really nice of you to say, Evan. You're a supernice guy, too." I was starting to get a little fed up with paying compliments all the time, but I couldn't stop. "So, what you're saying—in the nicest possible way, because you're so nice—is that I've screwed up here?"

"Well, yeah, but I'm not blaming you, 'cause I know your intentions were good. Anyway, you can fix this, can't you? Unwish it?"

"Yeah. 'Course," I said. "But—I need to think about how to do it."

"Yeah, it's a problem, all right."

As soon as he said that, I thought, *Oh no, no, no don't—*

Then everything went black.

Chapter Fifteen

I seemed to be floating somewhere. Not like when you're floating in water and you can feel yourself bobbing up and down. In fact, floating's probably the wrong word. I only say that because my feet weren't touching the ground. I don't think there was any ground to touch. Everything was black. I mean, *really* black. I closed my eyes and opened them again and it didn't make any difference. I had no idea where I was, or if I even was anywhere. I was fairly sure I wasn't in Sainsbury's anymore, but that was about all I *was* sure of.

"Evan?"

Silence.

"I wish I knew where I was."

You are apart from the world, the Wish-Answerer said. It was a relief to hear that serious news anchor's voice again. At least someone was talking to me.

"I wish I knew why I was here."

You wished for a world with no problems. But then you yourself faced the problem of what to wish for next. So you had to be removed from the world. To keep it free of problems. As you yourself had wished.

Well, that's exactly what I'd thought. Unless I wanted to spend the rest of my life dangling around here in the dark, I'd have to allow a few problems back into the world.

The wish about nobody dying—that would have to go, too. We didn't want *that* many problems. And the wish about everybody being nice all the time—well, that had been, er, nice in some ways, but you couldn't really keep going like that. Even just a day of it had started to give me the heebie-jeebies.

"All right," I said to the Wish-Answerer. "Here's what I wish. I want the world to go back to exactly how it was one second *before* I wished everyone was nice all the time and that people would stop dying, okay?"

The scene changed like a film cut. I was back in my bedroom, hovering around in zero grav, holding a glass of root beer with a straw in it. It was about seven in the evening. I could hear the dog barking out in the yard. Downstairs, the TV was on and I heard the toilet flush in the bathroom. The world was up and running again.

I finished the root beer, positioned myself above the bed, wished for gravity to return to normal, and plopped down onto the quilt.

Okay.

Now what?

It's fair to say I was feeling frazzled. Events of the last few days had been a little . . . *extreme*. I'd changed things so often and changed them back again that I hardly knew where I was anymore.

I had almost infinite power, but in a strange kind of way I felt almost powerless. Because I no longer had any direct contact with reality— it wasn't like I was a person *in* the world anymore, a person who could actually be affected by stuff that went on around me.

It was more like the world wasn't *real* to

me anymore. It was a world of LEGO pieces, or Play-Doh, that I could just remodel however I wanted.

I'd turned the world into a toy.

People who lose contact with reality are crazy, aren't they?

Insane.

And I have to say I was feeling pretty insane at this point.

Maybe I should ask the Wish-Answerer what to do? He was the only person—if he *was* a person—who seemed to know what was going on.

I had a sudden urge for a personal interview.

"Wish-Answerer? I wish you'd come and see me."

There was a sudden fierce heat.

This time it was its proper size: a rugged chunk of rock, about as big as a washing machine, standing there on skinny legs in the middle of my bedroom.

"I need some explanations, Wish-Answerer," I said. "What *are* you exactly?"

There is no word in your language for the kind of being I am.

"But you're alive, right? You're some sort of life-form?"

I'm still not sure how it did it, since it was one big chunk of rock, but the Meteor nodded.

"So you're not really a meteor?"

No. I merely resemble one.

"Why?"

You would not understand.

"And why—I mean, I wish you'd tell me why you gave me all those wishes."

You would not understand.

"Well, tell me anyway."

To renticufilicate the sparsunstrang of the universe.

"Oh. Yeah. Right. I thought it might be that."

I said you would not understand.

"Okay, look—whatever reason you did it for, you're on my side, right? You're here to help me?"

I do not take sides. But I am here to answer your wishes.

"I'm not sure I want the wishes anymore," I said, and as soon as I said it I realized it was true. Having all those wishes made life pointless. Even down to little things, like playing Wild Animals Top Trumps with Evan. It was no fun beating him when I knew what all his cards were. And the same went for soccer, or chess, or any game at all—there was no fun if you could just win without effort. Suppose I decided to run a marathon? As soon as I got tired I'd wish it was over, and I'd be at the finish line.

But it wasn't just sports and games. The whole of *life* made no sense. Life means struggling, learning, improving, practicing—*achieving* things. But you can't *achieve* anything when you only have to wish for it. All those things I'd wished to be amazing at—French and soccer and chess and Science—I couldn't actually *enjoy* them.

I opened my mouth. "I wish I wasn't amazing at French and soccer and chess and Science anymore—only just as good as I used to be."

To test myself I tried to think what the French word for *grapefruit* was, and realized I didn't know. So that was good. If I wanted to find out, I'd have to—well, find out.

But I hadn't solved anything in the long run. If you've got the wishes, you can't help using them. Nobody could resist it.

I took a deep breath, gulped, and said, "I wish I didn't have any more wishes."

I cannot grant that wish.

"What? Why can't you?"

It is in direct contradiction to your first wish. You cannot both have a million wishes and not have them. You wished for a million wishes. You must therefore have a million wishes.

"Then I wish I could go back in time to just before I wished for them and *not* wish for them!" I said. This seemed pretty cunning to me.

The Wish-Answerer gave a snuffling noise, as if it was laughing. *That's impossible*, it said. *A logical paradox.*

"Why?" I demanded. "I wished to go back in time before and that was okay!"

But you did not wish not to have your wishes. That cannot be. If you did not wish for the million wishes, then the wish to return to an earlier time and not have them could not be granted—because you would not be able, now, to wish!

"What?" A sick feeling began to steal over me. "But I thought I could wish for anything. I can break the laws of physics!"

But not the laws of logic, the Wish-Answerer said. *You have the wishes now, and there is only one logically consistent way to get rid of them.*

"Use them all up?"

That is correct.

"And how many have I had so far?"

One hundred and sixty-four.

Oh, well, wasn't that just terrific. That meant I had . . . actually, I couldn't be bothered to do the calculation so I just wished I knew the answer: nine hundred and ninety-nine thousand eight hundred and thirty-six.

Well, nine hundred and ninety-nine thousand eight hundred and thirty-five, now that

I'd used one up on the calculation. But that was still a boatload of wishes.

By the time I'd worked my way through them I'd be a gibbering wreck. And what sort of mess would the world be in?

"Oh, all right," I said, a bit moodily. "You might as well go then."

And the next instant, the Meteor was gone. No good-bye or catch you later or anything. Just . . . *pfft*. No more Meteor, except for a slight smell of smoke.

Chapter Sixteen

The sun was glowing above the trees, casting long, slanting shadows. I looked behind me and I seemed to be twenty yards tall again. Evan, too. And Billiam's shadow looked more like a giraffe's than a dog's.

It was a mild evening, about eight o'clock. Soon it would be dusk. I had that sort of sweet/sad feeling you sometimes get on fine, quiet autumn evenings. The trees were turning from green to yellow, and a few leaves were already falling. It was Friday, so no school the next day. Me and Evan had taken the dog out for a walk, to discuss the Wish Problem. I'd just explained to him all about what had happened—'cause of course he didn't remember any of that stuff about everyone being nice and nobody dying. As far as he was concerned, it hadn't happened.

"So you just unwished it all?"

"That's right."

"You're not—I mean, there's no danger you'll unwish about my dad being well again? 'Cause I couldn't bear it, really . . ."

"No, no, don't worry, I've got no reason to do that. What I need to do is get rid of the rest of the wishes without messing anything up too much. But nine hundred and ninety-nine thousand eight hundred and thirty-five . . ."

"That's a lot to get through," Evan agreed. "Can't you just think of some sort of pointless wish and keep making it, and run them down like that? Like, wish you were wearing a hat and then wish you weren't wearing it and then wish you were, and so on, till they run out?"

"Well, I *could* . . ." I was a little doubtful if this was going to use them up fast enough. "Lemme give it a try . . . I wish I was wearing a hat, I wish I wasn't wearing a hat, I wish I was wearing a hat, I wish I wasn't wearing a hat, I wish I was wearing a hat, I wish I wasn't wearing a hat, I wish I was wearing a hat, I wish I wasn't wearing a hat . . ." I stopped. It felt weird, this hat settling on my head and then vanishing over and over again. I could just see the brim of it. It was blue.

Evan was looking at me and laughing. "It looked like it was sort of flashing on and off—like the light on top of a police car."

"Well, that's eight wishes down. Nine hundred and ninety-nine thousand eight hundred and twenty-seven to go. But how long did it take?" I wished I knew. "Ten seconds. So it takes about a second to make a wish. To get rid of them all, that would take . . ." Again, I wished I knew the answer straight off. "That's over two hundred and seventy-seven hours. Or about eleven and a half days, nonstop, without eating or sleeping!"

"At least you just used up another couple of wishes figuring it out."

"Yeah, great, only nine hundred and ninety-nine thousand eight hundred and twenty-*five* to go. There's gotta be an easier way."

"Can't you just use them up a little more slowly? It might take a few weeks, but . . ."

I shook my head. "As long as I've got them I know I'm gonna use them. And every wish I make makes the world seem a little more unreal and pointless. I'll go crazy, Evan. Really."

I picked up a stick and threw it for Billiam. He went running after it, stirring up piles of fallen leaves.

Fallen leaves.

"Why don't you—" Evan began.

"Shush!" I said, waving my hand at him.

Fallen leaves.

My mind went into overdrive!

"Evan," I said slowly. "I think I've got it."

"What's the answer?" said Evan.

"It'll work," I said. "I'm sure it will."

"What?" demanded Evan.

"Are you listening, Meteor?" I said. "I want nine hundred and ninety-nine thousand eight hundred and twenty-four leaves to fall from the trees in this forest—and each fallen leaf counts as a wish gone. Okay?"

Okay, the voice of the Meteor said inside my head.

All around us, yellow leaves, detached by the breeze, fell, swirling and twirling and twisting to the ground.

Evan drew in his breath. He looked at me and grinned. "Oh, neat. Nice. Sweet."

"Yeah, it was pretty good, wasn't it?"

I'd saved my sanity! I could live a normal life again!

Normal, but better than before.

Everyone in my family was happy. Maeve with Stefan Bumgarner and Dad with his new job and Mom with her art exhibition and Ben with his lice-free scalp, magic helicopter, and new reading ability.

Evan had his dad back in tip-top health.

And as for me, I still had a million pounds stashed on top of the wardrobe.

"Just one thing, though," Evan said. "You wished for nine hundred and ninety-nine

thousand eight hundred and twenty-*four* leaves
to fall. I thought it was eight hundred and
twenty-*five*?"

"Oh, yeah, I'm keeping one wish in
reserve," I said. "For an emergency."

ABOUT THE AUTHOR

Brandon Robshaw has written several books for children, including some under the name of Adam Blade for the Beast Quest and Sea Quest series. He studied English literature at Oxford University before becoming a schoolteacher and university lecturer. Brandon lives in East London with his wife, three children, and dog.